No Smoke Without Flames

Geonn Cannon

Supposed Crimes LLC • Matthews, North Carolina

All Rights Reserved
Copyright © 2023 Geonn Cannon

Published in the United States.

ISBN: 978-1-952150-39-5

www.supposedcrimes.com

This book is typeset in Goudy Old Style.

No Smoke Without Flames

CHAPTER ONE

ON THE day they met, the love of Lea Contreras' life was wearing a yellow T-shirt that said SORRY I'M LATE, I DIDN'T WANT TO COME in big black letters.

The romance of the memory wasn't improved by the location, a loft space in the South Loop. It was a perpetually for-lease space with exposed brick and visually-impressive windows but not much else in its favor. An L train rattled the glass of the windows every ten minutes. The magazine that had hired Lea for this photoshoot rented it for cheap, and she had spent the past five hours parading a series of first responders in front of her camera.

"Are you Lee Contreras?"

"Le-ah," she corrected without looking up from her camera.

"Oh. There wasn't an H."

"I know. But it's..."

She looked up and was caught short by the woman walking toward her. Tall, close to six feet if not taller. Black hair cut short, but shaggy on top. Plaid shirt unbuttoned to show off the message underneath. Her jeans looked brand new, and they were tucked into the top of motorcycle boots. She was carrying a bag with her gear in it. Her sleeves were rolled up, and the sight of the flexed muscles in her forearms made Lea's stomach twist.

"Um. Ahem. It's how my parents wanted it," Lea finished, sweeping her hair back away from her face as she stepped forward.

"Victoria Branigan?"

"Yeah. Tori." She didn't look happy about it, like she hoped this was a case of mistaken identity. "They said I could change here."

Lea pointed toward a side office they'd been using for hair and makeup. "In there."

Tori didn't move.

"We're on the clock." Lea kept her voice neutral, not angry. "If we lose the sun, we'll have to set up lights, and you'll be here a lot longer."

"Right. Okay." She turned toward the changing room. "You're not going to trick me, right?"

Lea frowned. "Trick you how?"

"They said I would be in my uniform the entire time. You're not going to take a few normal pictures and then suggest maybe we get one or two with my shirt off 'just to see how it looks', are you?"

Lea had a pretty good idea how it would look. She tried not to picture it. "This isn't that kind of magazine. Everyone has been in their uniforms the entire time."

Tori nodded. "Okay. It's just..." She shrugged. "Female firefighters. I feel like when people think of us, they still expect the sexy Halloween version."

"Ah. Well, let's do what we can to change the narrative, hm?"

Tori went to change and came back in her uniform. Like the paramedics, police officers, nurses, and EMTs before her, she assumed an awkward pose with her hands folded in front of her. She kept her back straight and her chin up like she was getting her passport photo taken. Tori took a picture just to be polite, but then lowered the camera and moved closer.

"So what made you decide to join the fire department?"

"I was an athlete in high school. I loved track-and-field, basketball. I wanted a job that would force me to stay active."

Lea nodded. "Makes sense. It seems like most women get into it because of a family history."

"Legacies, yeah. That happens a lot," Tori admitted. "But my dad worked for the post office. Mom teaches second grade. My sisters both think I'm nuts."

"What do they do?"

"One manages a grocery store, the other is a veterinarian. My mom says we all save the world in different ways."

Lea smiled. "She's not wrong. But I think you've got a leg up in the hero department, running into burning buildings and all."

"I'll let you make that argument to them."

She had relaxed slightly, dropping her hands to her sides. Lea took the opening.

"Can you move your right foot toward me a little? That's perfect. Turn a little... yes. Now lower your chin? Good, perfect." She snapped another picture. "In a second I want to get a couple with your helmet, if that's okay."

"Anything that hides my face."

Lea shook her head. "Visor stays up. We're going to want to see those hazel eyes."

Tori said, "Most people say brown."

"Are they brown?"

"No. They're hazel. But most people just assume."

Lea shook her head. "No, no. I like to be precise. Color is important. And hazel eyes are rare. You have to appreciate them, especially when they're as lovely as yours."

Tori blinked. "Thanks-thank you."

"Sure." She brought the camera up. She snapped a picture, then lowered the camera just enough that she could look over the viewfinder. "Can we get one with you crouching? Arms on your thighs? I just want to see how it will look."

"Sure." She moved her feet apart and bent her knees. The pose wasn't quite as intimidating as Lea had hoped, but she snapped a few angles anyway just in case she changed her mind. "How about you? Family of photographers?"

"God, no. My parents thought it was a nice hobby, but they told me only possible career path would be weddings and bar mitzvahs."

Tori said, "But you proved them wrong."

"I did. There are a lot of bat mitzvahs, too."

Tori actually smiled at that, and Lea took a picture before it could escape. "You have a wonderful smile. We should get some shots of it."

"I felt like this should probably be more serious."

"Okay. We can be serious if you want."

Tori considered it. "I don't know."

The train sped by again, shaking the whole loft.

"Well, you can take your time. We don't have to decide right now."

"What about losing the sunlight?"

Lea shrugged. "We can take as long as it takes for you to feel comfortable with the pictures."

She saw Tori's shoulders relax. "Sounds good to me. Let's see what happens."

What happened was another twenty minutes of photos, the best of which came from the end of the session. Tori became more relaxed, more animated, as she talked about herself. The tension faded from her posture and Lea caught a half dozen candid moments she thought would be perfect for the article. Eventually the sun got low enough in the sky that they had to end the shoot. Tori actually looked disappointed when Lea told her she was free to go.

"Did you get what you needed?"

She'd gotten more than enough, actually. "You really loosened up at the end. We got some really great options. Do you want to go through them?"

"No, definitely not. I'll trust your judgement."

Lea nodded. "Okay. It will be the magazine making the final decision, but I'll send them enough that they'll have a lot to choose from. And if you leave me an email or something, I can send you the rest. It's always good to have nice pictures of yourself."

"I suppose. Thank you." Tori hesitated. "It's strange. I spent the past two weeks dreading this. And now that it's over, I feel like I want it to keep going."

"Like dragging yourself into bed at night–"

"And dragging yourself out in the morning." Tori grinned. "Exactly."

Lea tapped her finger on the edge of her camera. "You know, if you're interested... I mean, there's a coffee place down the street. We could go there. Keep talking. If you want."

"That would be great. My stuff..."

"You can keep it in my truck."

Tori nodded. "That would be great. I'll just go change."

When she came back, her shirt was buttoned up to cover the DIDN'T WANT TO COME message. Lea didn't know if it meant anything, but she smiled when she saw Tori had taken the effort to cover it up.

It was full dark by the time they reached the street. Tori put her uniform in the back of Lea's truck with the camera equipment. Lea pointed her in the right direction for the coffee shop. Tori put her hands in the back pockets of her jeans and watched her feet. Lea wrapped her arms around herself and looked up at the tracks overhead, an iron framework that stretched from one side of the street to the other.

"So I guess I might as well get the obvious questions out of the way now, before I go too far down the wrong path." Tori looked at Lea. "Gay?"

Lea laughed. "Yeah. Single?"

"Available," Tori said.

"That's the same thing, isn't it?"

Tori shook her head. "Not really. Someone can be single and totally uninterested in pursuing a relationship. Someone can be in a relationship and looking for something better. 'Available' bridges the gap a little. But to be totally transparent, I'm not in a relationship right now. I'm open to the possibility of one. Under the right circumstances."

Lea nodded. "That makes sense. I'm available, too."

"Good. Not that..." She laughed nervously. "I still would want to get coffee and spend time with you, even if that wasn't the case. You're interesting. You'd be interesting even if you weren't available."

Lea laughed. "That's nice. I'm glad you find me objectively interesting and that you consider me a potential date. I've got all my bases covered."

"Yeah," Tori said.

"The same goes for you... obviously. Beautiful firefighter amazon."

Tori laughed. "Wow. Thank you. The, uh, clumsy six-foot nerd I was in high school just did a backflip."

"Clumsy? You said you were an athlete."

"I was! I could run, I could throw a ball. Put me on a track or a court, and I was untouchable, especially after I had a growth spurt in eighth grade. Not so much in a hallway with a hundred other kids who were usually a foot shorter than me. High schools were not built for kids my size."

"I guess that's true. It's easier when you're puny like me. Easier to blend in that way."

When they got to the coffee shop, there was a brief battle over which of them would pay. Tori won, only because her arms were longer and it was easier for her to hand the cash to the barista before Lea could stop her. "I'll owe you one," Lea said, deciding not to dwell on the implications of the comment.

The tables were all occupied, so Tori suggested they keep walking with the coffees. Now Lea was the one who didn't want the day to end. She scrolled through her mental catalogue of conversation topics to prevent any lulls that might bring the night to an end.

"I don't want to ask what I'm sure *everyone* asks you..."

"Cool fire stories?" Tori guessed.

Lea smiled sheepishly. "You probably get sick of talking about it. Fires are scary. And it's your job. So hey, okay. How about this? What's a really cool thing you got to do that has nothing to do with fighting fires?"

"Like saving kittens from trees?"

Lea snapped her head around, eyes wide. "Really?"

Tori laughed. "No. I've never saved a cat from a tree, unfortunately. I think that's just a myth."

"Damn. But no, yeah, I meant... there have to be perks."

"Sure. I like going to elementary schools and talking to the kids. It can be a little annoying when I feel cynical, because I know I'm playing the token female sent out to make the department look good. But I love those days. The kids look at me like I'm Wonder Woman. It's great."

Lea nodded. "I'll bet."

"What about you? Fun photography jobs that are about more than a paycheck."

Lea sighed. "I don't know, honestly. I haven't really done anything just for my portfolio in a long time. That's the problem with doing what you love. After a while it just becomes a job like anything else."

"That's depressing."

Lea shrugged. "I still find joy in it. Taking pictures, finding a perfect shot. But it's not the same as it used to be when it's how I pay the bills."

"That makes sense."

"You made it fun today," Lea said. "More fun than it's been in a long time. I appreciate that."

Tori said, "I'm glad we could make it a good experience for each other, then."

Lea nodded. They stopped at a corner. If they continued across the street, they could go into Millennium Park and continue meandering for as long as they wanted. If they turned left, they could circle around the building and return to where Lea's truck was parked. Tori could get her stuff and say goodbye, and they would probably never see each other again.

The crosswalk sign changed. Tori nodded at the crosswalk. "Want to go into the park?"

Lea exhaled softly, relieved without realizing she'd been stressed, and nodded.

The light changed when they were halfway across. They both quickened their step, and Tori reached back and took Lea's hand as if it was the most natural thing in the world. Lea accepted the grip without saying anything and let herself be pulled onto the opposite side of the street. Tori let go and looked down as her hand dropped back to her side.

"Sorry. Shit. That was just instinct."

"It's fine. I didn't mind."

They walked into the park together. The Bean loomed to their right, and Tori led the way toward the plaza in front of the sculpture.

"You know I've never actually been here?" Lea admitted.

"Really? How long have you lived in Chicago?"

"I never really saw the appeal. It's a big shiny bean." She shook her head as she looked at it. "Why? It would make sense in Boston." She looked up at the shiny curves, where a distorted version of the skyline created a bright line across the center. "It's kind of pretty at night, I guess."

"You know it's not actually called the Bean, right? That's just a nickname."

"It makes more sense than Cloud Gate."

"No, it... it's supposed to be a bridge between land and sky," Tori said. "It reflects the sky and brings it down to the ground level. It twists things. The sky is down here, we're up there..." She realized Lea was staring at her and pressed her lips together. "I don't know. That's just how I've always thought of it."

Lea smiled and looked up at the sculpture again. "When you look at it like that, I guess... it's really amazing after all. It's beautiful, actually."

Tori bit her bottom lip and tilted her head back as they got closer to the sculpture. Their mirrored duplicates were dark silhouettes on the steel surface. It was harder to notice their height difference like this, which was another aspect that Lea could appreciate.

"Do you want to get dinner?"

"Now?" Tori took out her phone to check the time. "I usually don't eat until later. Is there a place around here that's good?"

Lea spoke quickly, getting the words out before she regretted them. "It doesn't have to be now. Or tonight. I'd like to buy you dinner."

Tori looked at her. "Oh. Like a date."

"Yeah. I'm asking you out on a date. I don't really know what's happening here. But I know that I'll be more relaxed about saying goodnight if I know I get to see you again at some point in the future. And I don't want to make 'friend' plans and pretend like I'd be okay with that. Unless the date doesn't go well. In which case I would be fine just being your friend. But I want to see if there's potential before I settle for that."

Tori nodded slowly. Her eyes were wide and she had a shell-shocked smile on her face.

"That was a lot," Lea admitted.

"It was. But it was nice. I liked it." She looked around and then started to slowly nod. "I would love to get dinner with you sometime. I'd be okay with you as a friend, too. I don't have a lot of friends, and I think you'd be a good one."

Lea heard that as a rejection of the other option, and nodded. "Okay. That's—"

"But we'll see how the date goes. Before we... label anything."

"Okay," Lea said.

They looked up at the Bean again.

Lea moved her hand, felt it bump against Tori's, and turned her wrist until their palms were touching. Tori looked down and slipped her fingers between Lea's. Lea kept her eyes on the curved steel reflecting the night sky back at them.

It wasn't such a bad sculpture after all, she decided.

Six months later, on a sunny Saturday, Lea and Tori returned to the Cloud Gate. This time the plaza was crowded with tourists taking photos from every conceivable angle. Lea took Tori's hand again and got down on one knee.

"What are you doing?" Tori asked in a tone that indicated she knew the answer.

"Victoria Branigan..."

"Get up."

Lea's heart was pounding too hard for her to hear. She'd planned this moment for so long, and to such intricate detail, that she couldn't process anything that might throw a wrench in her script.

"Will you marry me?"

Tori pressed her lips together and looked around, scanning the crowd like she was worried they would be called as witnesses.

"Lea..."

Her smile wavered. "Tori...?"

"Get up. Please, babe."

Lea awkwardly got up off her knee. Blood was rushing in her ears but she distinctly heard the voice of an elderly woman nearby say, "Oh no... honey, stop, don't film."

"No?" Lea said under her breath.

"Not... not 'no'," Tori said. "I thought we talked about this..."

Lea let Tori's hands drop. "We did. But... I thought that there... that we..."

"Let's talk about this at home, okay?"

"No," Lea said, backing away. "No, I don't... think we... uh, we can..." She waved her hand in front of her face like she was trying to swat a fly. "I think I need to go f-for a walk."

She turned and walked away. She saw the elderly couple fumbling with their phone. They had probably seen her get down on one knee and tried to get a video of the moment. Now they were trying to act like they hadn't seen anything. Lea turned her face away from them and rubbed the heel of her hand against her eyes, half-running to get away from the plaza before word of her humiliation could spread to the entire group.

Tori caught up with her on the other side of the pavilion. "Lea, stop. Please, stop. Let's talk."

"Talk?" Lea was openly crying now. "What is there to talk about? Have you ever heard of a relationship surviving a failed marriage proposal?"

"I'm positive it happens all the time." Tori put a hand on Lea's shoulder. "Please."

Lea stopped walking but didn't face her.

"I thought I was clear about how I felt," Tori said softly. "About marriage, a-about everything."

"Things seemed... different." She sniffled and wiped at her eyes, suddenly aware of the people who were giving them a wide berth. "I can't believe I humiliated myself in public like that."

"You didn't do anything wrong." Tori put her hands on Lea's shoulders. "You took a chance. I'm sorry I didn't react the way you hoped. But being against marriage and ceremonies doesn't mean I'm unhappy. I still want to be with you. And I plan to be with you for a long time. But I want it to be a choice I make, not a decision I'm locked into."

Lea took a deep breath. "I'm not trying to trap you."

"I know."

"If you end up in the hospital—"

"I know," Tori said. "And I hope you know this has nothing to do with how I feel about you. I love you. If I *was* going to marry someone, it would be you. I never said no back there."

Lea raised an eyebrow. "You didn't say yes."

Tori nodded and looked down. "I didn't want to slam the door. My answer isn't a hard no. My answer is that I don't know. I don't know if I want that. And it wouldn't be fair to you if I just went through the motions and hated every second of it. I just want to be with you. I want to be yours. And I want to prove that to you every day without wasting thousands of dollars on a ceremony and filing a paper with the state."

"But it's more than that. You understand that, right?" Lea was desperate now. "Marriage isn't just... just like registering your car."

"Yeah. I know."

Lea stepped away from Tori and looked out over the pavilion. Tori stayed where she was, giving Lea room to breathe.

"Can... can you at least say you'll consider changing your mind? Reconsidering?"

Tori said, "Lea Contreras... nothing has ever made me reconsider marriage more than knowing you want to be married to me. So of course I'll reconsider. And maybe my opinions will change in time. If anyone can make me switch camps, it would be you."

Lea nodded. "Okay."

"Is that enough?"

"It's enough for now."

Tori held her arms out. Lea went to her, and they hugged tightly.

"I love you, Victoria."

Tori kissed Lea's hair. "I love you too, Lea. I don't need a ring or a contract to prove it. I'm going to prove it to you every day."

Lea pressed her cheek into Tori's shoulder and nodded, since she didn't trust her voice to sound convincing at the moment.

It was enough. She truly believed it was enough.

For now.

The door opened with a hellish creak, and everyone in the courtroom turned to look at her. An older woman stood at a podium directly ahead of her at the other side of the room. Lea was standing next to her, and Tori's sister Elizabeth was standing on the other side. Tori wanted to shrink down into the collar of her dress shirt. It actually took all her willpower to keep her hands at her sides, because they wanted to lift up the lapel of her blazer and tug it up over her face. Instead she smiled sheepishly and walked quickly down the aisle between two banks of empty seats.

"You're cutting it a little close," Elizabeth said.

Tori shrugged. "You're not supposed to see the bride before the wedding, right?" She turned to Lea and bent down to kiss her cheek. "You look amazing," she whispered before she stepped back.

"You too," Lea said, admiring Tori's suit. "I was half-afraid you'd show up in that 'didn't want to come' shirt."

Tori had actually considered it, just as a joke. But the text had faded from too many washings, and she felt the day deserved a little more respect.

The judge cleared her throat. "Are we ready?"

"We're ready," Tori said. "Sorry. I was..." She waved off her excuse. "Yeah, we're ready."

"Then let's begin."

Tori took her position in front of the podium and took Lea's hands in hers.

Three years earlier, she had walked into a building that looked abandoned and discovered a treasure buried there. Lea Contreras, funny and brilliant and incredibly talented. Shy, but fierce when defending her loved ones. Tori was impressed with her immediately and, by the time they parted ways at the end of the night, was incredibly fond of her. A series of dates over the next month turned fondness into something deeper. Something even a commitment-phobic person like Tori couldn't deny.

But there were lines she still couldn't cross. Her heart had leapt into her throat when Lea got down on one knee. There was no ring - Lea knew how Tori felt about any kind of jewelry, especially "symbolic ownership rings" - but the intention was clear even before she said the words.

When Tori's captain discovered she'd turned down the

proposal, he threatened to demote her to probie and assign her every shit job he could think of until she made things right.

"That girl adores you," he said, throwing a chip at her across the dinner table. "And I know you love her more than anything. You're good together. So what the hell are you waiting for? A better offer? Call her right now and tell her you changed your mind."

Tori couldn't do it. She and Lea spent many nights discussing it, arguing, crying, until they came to an understand.

Then two years later, a firefighter was killed by a roof collapse during a fire Tori was also working. She was safe outside the building when everything came crashing down, but in the aftermath she couldn't stop playing the 'what if' game in her head. She called Lea from the hospital.

"I'm okay."

Lea sobbed into the phone, too relieved to form words.

"I'll marry you."

"What?" A sniffle.

"I don't want..." She looked down at her boots. She still reeked of smoke. Her hand was shaking. "If something had happened to me... I don't... I don't..." She had started crying at some point during the call. "Partner and girlfriend. Neither of them sounds permanent. If something happens to me, I want them to call my wife. I want them to let my wife in to see me."

Lea sniffled again. "You want to marry me in case you die?"

Tori winced. "No. I'm, I'm explaining it wrong. Jerry just died, Lea. I don't know what I'm saying or thinking or..." She pinched the bridge of her nose. "I just know what I want. And I want you to be my wife. If you're going to be anything to me, it should be something permanent."

There was silence on the line between them. Finally, Lea said, "Am I an awful person for wanting to wait for a better proposal before I answer?"

Tori laughed and wiped her eyes. "That's fair. I'm sorry I made you wait so long."

"I'm glad you didn't give in. I didn't want to badger you into saying yes. I wanted you to want to say yes. And it doesn't have to be a huge wedding or a big dumb ceremony. It can be as small as you want it to be. The wedding is the least important part to me."

"Good. I'd look terrible in a dress."

Lea laughed. "I'm so glad you're okay. I love you."

"I love you, too." She looked down the hall where the rest of the company was starting to gather. "I should go be with the guys."

"Yeah. I'll wa~"

"Don't wait up. I might be late, so let me wake you."

"Okay. Be safe."

"I will. Goodnight, Lea."

"Goodnight, Victoria."

She'd hung up and went to grieve with the rest of her team, her family. The next morning, Lea held her while she cried and stayed with her until she finally fell asleep. When she woke up in the afternoon, they talked about the phone call. Tori had slipped off the bed and knelt on the floor. She cupped Lea's face in her hands and stared into her eyes.

"Will you marry me?"

"Yes."

And now here they were. The date had seemed so far away when they set it, and now it was almost in the past. She had been Lea Contreras' wife for almost an entire day before she realized the woman lying beside her in bed was now officially named Lea Branigan. There were no rings, no gifts, not even an official announcement in the paper. Just a name-change form and a piece of paper declaring they were betrothed.

"Are you okay?" Lea asked.

"Fantastic." She tightened her arm around Lea to draw her closer. "I'm just thinking how weird it is that I'm married."

Lea lifted her head. "It's not that different from yesterday, is it?"

"I guess not," Tori admitted. "The day feels different, of course. It feels monumental."

"It's like a birthday," Lea said, putting her head back down. "You acknowledge the date, it feels special and magical, but the next day you don't feel a year older."

Tori nodded. "Right."

"So nothing really has to change."

Tori relaxed. She had been so worried that just going through with the act, even without the church or minister, would trigger some kind of flight response in her mind. But Lea was right. It felt like any other night lying next to the woman she loved. She certainly couldn't have asked for a better partner.

She reached for the lamp and turned it off, then curled onto her side so they were facing each other. Lea sighed happily and brushed her nose against Tori's.

Maybe there was a chance she would enjoy being married after all.

Chapter Two

Three Years Later

JANICE KOZAK stood in the doorway of her restaurant's kitchen, arms crossed, and watched as the firefighters finished up. The fire had been relatively small. She'd been spared any major damage to the fixtures. But the smoke had been tremendous, which set off the smoke alarms, which meant the fire department had to come out and screw up her afternoon. She had to shut down while they made sure everything was safe to continue using.

Her restaurant, Canvas, was still relatively new to the neighborhood. They'd only been open for six months. They had been getting decent reviews online, a handful of glowing reviews, and they already had a couple of people they considered regulars. But foot traffic was their bread and butter, so to speak, and she'd been dreading the idea of shutting down for an extended period. Fortunately the firefighter in charge already revealed weren't going to keep her closed. The fire had been out by the time they arrived and the damage was minimal. Now they just seemed to be poking around to justify the trip.

Of course it wasn't all bad. The firefighter that had been talking the most was a woman, and a gorgeous woman at that. Janice was furious at her cook - *former* cook - for causing the mess, but it was almost worth the hassle to see this goddess up close. The back of her coat said BRANIGAN. Janice liked that name. It was a very strong name. The firefighter turned and caught her looking, smiled apologetically.

"We shouldn't be too much longer, ma'am."

"I know you're just making sure everything is safe, off~" She caught herself. "Are you called officers, or is that just cops?"

She smiled. "You can just call me Tori."

"In that case, it's Janice instead of ma'am."

"Fair enough." Tori's smile brightened her whole face. She looked around the kitchen. "So what kind of food do you serve here?"

"American bistro." At Tori's blank look, Janice smiled and clarified. "Burgers, chicken, steaks, that sort of thing."

Tori nodded. "Well, it smells delicious."

"You can smell it through all the smoke stink?"

"Years of training," Tori said with a wink.

Janice was intrigued by that win. She stood up straighter. "You should come by and try us out sometime. We're usually pretty slow on Wednesdays. You can be my VIP for the night."

Tori nodded. "That sounds possible." Her eyebrows shot up and she tilted her head to the side, opening her mouth slightly as if she'd just had a great idea. "Wednesdays? Like this Wednesday?"

"Uh, sure," Janice said. "I can pencil in a reservation to make sure we have a table set aside. Just in case. Eight o'clock?"

"Perfect," Tori said. "Yeah. That would be great."

Janice was too surprised to react properly. Her irritation with the afternoon faded away as thoughts of Wednesday took precedence.

Tori Branigan and the other firefighters were gone fifteen minutes later. Evan, her kitchen manager, came out of the office once the coast was clear. He was taller than her, taller than any of the other employees, in fact. He wore thick black-rimmed glasses and had a shock of white hair that made him look like a rooster as he craned his neck down to look out the pass-through into the dining room. He raised his eyebrows at her as he straightened back up.

"Everything okay to open for dinner?"

"Yeah, they signed off on everything. We can open right now."

He snapped the fingers of both hands, his version of clapping. He started to walk away from her, then turned back. "I heard you talking to that lady fireman."

"Shut up," she said.

"I heard you make a date with that lady fireman," he said as he pushed the kitchen door open with his shoulder.

"I told you to shut up!" she laughed.

"Was she hot?" he called over his shoulder as he crossed the dining room.

Janice sighed and, knowing how stupid it would sound, said it anyway. "She was smoking."

Wednesday night arrived. Janice told herself she wasn't going to make a big deal about Firefighter Tori when she showed up. Okay, so she had dressed up very nice for the occasion. And yes, she may have reserved the nicest table in the restaurant. But this was *her* restaurant, and she could orchestrate every part of the evening to be as impressive as possible. She didn't know what Tori would order, but she asked her most trusted cook - Lily - to come in on her night off so all the potential bases would be covered.

At seven o'clock, Janice went to the front of the restaurant to seat guests. Evan looked knowingly at her over the rims of his glasses - she *never* seated guests - but he said nothing.

Janice perked up every time the door opened. She had been doing this job too long to let herself look disappointed whenever someone else appeared. She handed out menus, escorted the customers to their seats, and then hurried back to her position. Every time she hoped the next arrival would be the one she was waiting for.

She was on her way back from seating a couple when the door opened and Tori stepped inside. Even without her firefighter gear, it was undeniably her. She was wearing a large puffy coat and a knit cap. Janice realized this was the second time she'd seen the woman and she still didn't know what color her hair was. Tori stopped next to the hostess stand, slowly scanning the tables.

Janice quickened her pace toward the front of the restaurant. "You made it!"

Tori looked at her. She smiled.

The restaurant door opened and another woman came in. Shorter, dark-haired, tugging at a scarf wrapped around her neck.

Tori turned toward the new arrival and reached out. She carefully pulled at the scarf with one hand, lifting the end with her other, and effortlessly freed the smaller woman from its noose.

Oh no. Janice slowed down. For the first time that night, her smile faltered. *Oh shit oh no.*

Both women faced her. Tori draped the other woman's scarf over her own forearm.

"Hi. Sorry, we're a little late."

"Only a few minutes," Janice said without looking at the clock. She grabbed a pair of menus from the hostess stand, switching gears to treat them like any other guests.

"It's Janice, right?" Tori said. "This is my wife, Lea."

Disappointment twisted in Janice's gut. "Hi, Lea. I, um..." She gestured for them to follow her and started walking. "I have a table right over here for y-you."

Tori put a hand on Lea's shoulder to guide her through the dining room. "Is everything okay? We said Wednesday, right? If we're~"

"No, no, you're absolutely right. I was just distracted by, ah, you know. Work things. Always a hundred fires to put out." She laughed nervously. "So to speak."

"Right," Tori chuckled.

Tori sat with her back to the kitchen. Her wife sat across from her in the seat Janice had expected to take. Janice cleared her throat and gave her head a quick shake to clear it. Whatever she'd been planning and plotting about the past few days was now impossible. There was no use dwelling on it. Tori had been a nice fantasy for a while but she wouldn't, couldn't spend any more energy on it.

"So can I start you off with some drinks?"

Lea ordered a South Side cocktail, Tori ordered the house IPA. Janice assured them that both were excellent choices, slipping back into her professional groove.

"Take a second to look over the menu. And don't even look at the prices. Everything tonight is on the house."

"Oh!" Tori skimmed the prices. "*Oh.* That's really too generous."

"Not at all. I don't have out VIP titles for nothing." She winked at Lea. "I'll have those drinks right out."

She kept her smile in place until she was safely in the kitchen. She slumped against the wall behind the door and fake-sobbed.

Evan looked at the clock, then at her. "I thought you were supposed to be on your date."

"We decided to take it slow," Janice said. "For now I'll just stay miserable and alone, and she'll stay with her wife."

Evan hissed through his teeth. "Ouch. That's never fun. Do

you want Lily to undercook whatever they end up getting? I can order Lily to do it. I have that power."

"No," Janice sighed, pushing away from the wall. She went to make Lea's cocktail. "It was my own dumb fault. Jumping to conclusions, getting my hopes up."

"I always look for a ring before I start getting excited."

"She was at work! And wearing gloves for a lot of it. I think." She tried to remember if she had actually looked for a ring. "Whatever. It doesn't matter now. I'm taking this as a learning opportunity."

Evan shook his head. "Learning opportunities don't get you laid."

"Don't I know it," she grunted.

She took the cocktail, grabbed Tori's IPA from the cooler, and headed back out.

There was a bright side she could look at. Wife was a definite line in the sand. A girlfriend might be transient, casual, on the verge of ending. A girlfriend would have left her with a tiny thread of hope to hold onto. But wife? A wife was a commitment. A wife was a concrete wall.

It was better to have the bucket of cold water dumped on her this early before any real feelings could have set root.

Janice had completely redefined the night in her mind by the time Tori and Lea's food was ready. It was no longer a failed date, a miscommunication, a disaster. It was now exactly what Tori had assumed it would be. Janice was a friendly restaurant owner who supported the local fire department and wanted to show gratitude to someone who helped in a time of need. It didn't have to be a disaster just because it couldn't become anything more than that.

She took the plates out herself, a thinly-veiled excuse to get another look at the couple. It was clear that she wasn't even Tori's type. She was pale, blonde, blue-eyed, and more than a few people had pointed out she had 'angry eyes.' Lea, on the other hand, was Latina, with big doe eyes, and at the moment she was smiling like she was amused by the whole world. Tori said something just as Janice approached the table, and Lea put both hands flat on the table and leaned back in her chair to laugh. It was such an easy, casual laugh that Janice knew it would be impossible to hate someone who laughed like that.

"I hope you ladies aren't having too much fun over here."

Tori sat up straighter as Janice put the plate down in front of her. "Absolutely not."

"We're bored to tears," Lea said, still chuckling.

"I can see that," Janice said with a smile. "Let me know if I can get you anything else."

She returned to the kitchen. Evan stopped what he was doing long enough to give her a polite golf clap.

"Well done on being the bigger woman."

"I didn't have a chance," Janice said. "The wife is adorable *and* sexy. That combination should be illegal. And her eyes are green. *Green.* That's just not fair."

Evan sighed and leaned against the prep counter. "Look, fire lady is an Amazon, right? She's tall and muscular and she could throw any of us over her shoulder and carry us out of the building at the drop of a hat. You? You're a Viking warrior. Everyone in this room is terrified of you. Ask anyone. Jane!"

A waitress on the other side of the pass-through stopped. She couldn't see Janice in her current position. "Yeah?"

"Are you scared of Janice?"

She hesitated as she took her plate. "Why, is she mad at me?"

"No, you're good. Go back to work." He held his hands out to Janice. "See? Vikings and Amazons don't mix. They need the cute and perky one for balance. You and the fire lady would just growl and butt heads and tear each other apart within six months."

Janice's shoulders slumped. "But Amazons are hot."

"Yes, dear, I know, we all remember that you saw *Wonder Woman* seven times in the theater. I'm not saying the six months wouldn't be fun. I'm just saying..." He pointed. "That is not your Gal Gadot. But she's out there somewhere. You just have to keep looking."

Janice sighed and went back to her office.

She was just so damn sick of looking.

When the meal was finished, Janice made her way over to the table to try tempting them with dessert. Tori held up her hands in surrender while Lea shook her head with a remorseful smile.

"I wish I could use the free meal as an excuse to say yes to having more, but I need to be good." She sighed and patted her stomach. "It was delicious. Thank you."

"Sure, you're very welcome. Come back any time."

Lea said, "We definitely will." She leaned forward and started getting her coat back on. With one arm in the sleeve, she gestured at the walls. "I really like your art."

"Oh." Janice looked at it as if she'd only just noticed it hanging there. "Thank you. It's the best of a small selection, sadly. When I was fitting the place out, I was focused on getting the important fixtures right. Tables, chairs, silverware, you know. It was the day before we opened and I realized how horrible the walls looked without anything on them. A restaurant with a name like Canvas and there's no art on the walls... ridiculous, right?" She shrugged, embarrassed. "So I went to a couple of thrift stores and secondhand shops and got what I could."

Tori laughed. "You chose well, I think."

"Thank you. One of these days I want to hire a photographer to take pictures around town. You know, decorate with a little character."

Tori had frozen half out of her seat, lifting her head to look across the table. Lea was sitting up straighter. If human ears could actually prick up like a dog, hers would be standing straight up.

"What did I say?" Janice asked.

"I'm a photographer," Lea said, putting a hand on her chest. "I would love to help you out."

Janice raised her eyebrows. "Oh, really? Wow. I couldn't pay you much..."

"You just gave us a free meal. I think we could work something out," Lea said.

"That would be amazing." Janice was genuinely touched by the offer. She'd resigned herself to the mediocre artwork. "Thank you so much."

"Of course! I love the idea of my work hanging in a restaurant where everyone can see it." She looked around the room as if envisioning the finished product. "I've lived here my whole life. I know the parts of Chicago that will really make the locals feel at home here. We can find just the right things to create a, um..." She snapped her fingers at Tori.

"Ambiance."

"The ambiance you want, yes." She grinned, her eyes sparkling. "I'm excited!"

Janice laughed. "I can tell." She took a card from her apron. "This has my personal cell on it. We'll figure out a time that we're both free. Text first so I can put you in my phone."

Lea took the card. "Fantastic. That fire really worked out well for everybody, hm!"

Tori laughed. "It's always nice when fires bring people together." She held out her hand to Janice. "It really was a great meal. We'll definitely be back. And paying full price."

"If you insist."

Janice took Tori's strong, warm hand in hers. After all the mental buildup she'd given to this night, she would have expected ending it with a handshake would be a huge disappointment. But the promise of finally completing her restaurant's atmosphere had her too excited.

Lea surprised her with a hug. "Sorry, I'm a hugger," she said after the hug had already ended.

"That's fine. Be sure to tell your friends about us."

"Absolutely," Lea promised.

She walked them to the door. When she got back to the kitchen, Evan was waiting by the door.

"How much of that did you see?"

"Enough to see that you lost the love of your life but you gained a pair of insufferable couple friends."

She grunted at him as she went into the kitchen. He followed her.

"How long do you think before they start setting you up with their other single friends?"

Janice scoffed at the thought, then lifted her hands in surrender. "Hey, if their single friends look anything like them, sign me up."

CHAPTER THREE

"SHE WANTED you, you know."

"What? Who, Janice?" Tori lifted her head off the pillow. They were lying in bed, Tori's side dark while Lea's lamp was still on. She was casually thumbing through an art book, her glasses perched on the tip of her nose.

"Mm-hmm. I was thinking about taking her on a tour of street art." She lifted the book so Tori could see the cover. "There are so many gorgeous murals all over town. It would be the essence of Chicago without being too touristy or kitschy, you know? Staying away from, you know, Navy Pier and the Chicago Theatre."

"Okay," Tori said. "That sounds great. But what do you mean about her wanting me?"

Lea said, "Did you not see her face when we walked in? The change between when she saw you versus when she saw me right behind you?" She propped herself up on her elbow and demonstrated. "Happy and excited..." She lifted her eyebrows and smiled like a kid at Disney World. "Confusion." The smile faded, the brow furrowed. "Realization." Her whole face fell. "Distress... and then for the finish, a big, big fake smile." She widened her eyes and showed all her teeth.

Tori laughed at the demonstration. "You're reading too much into it."

"Victoria," Lea said, playfully stern. "She panicked when she saw me. Did you do anything special when you put out her fire? Save a kitten, maybe?"

"No. We didn't even have to put the fire out. It was just a little flare-up. It was out by the time we got there, so we just made sure the equipment was safe and undamaged."

Lea raised an eyebrow. "And for this, she gave you a free dinner. You saw those prices, Tori. She wasn't rewarding a hero firefighter. She was asking you out on a *date*."

"I'm positive she wasn't."

"What were her exact words when she invited you?"

"I don't remember her *exact* words. It was something like... I should come try the place out, and I could be her VIP for the night."

Lea dropped back onto her pillow and laughed, covering her face with both hands. "Vic-tor-i-ah!"

"What!"

"That... was... a... date. And your wife crashed it." She put her hands on her cheeks in mock horror. "I feel like such a fool. I won't stand in your way."

"No." Tori looked completely lost. "If... no, no. I-I didn't ask... s-she... I didn't know she was flirting with me, Lea."

Lea put her hands down. "Oh, honey. On one hand, I'm glad you're so dense because it kept you single long enough for me to find you. But it's still a little sad."

"So she was really asking me out?"

"Yes, darling." She sat up, took off her glasses and set them on the bedside table. She scooted closer to Tori and kissed her cheek. "As hard as it might be to believe, she was attracted to the beautiful, strong, charming firefighter."

Tori turned her head so their lips met, and Lea took the invitation to climb on top of her. After kissing for a while, Lea sat up to take off her pajama top.

"Seriously, though. How did you ever get laid before we met?"

"Sometimes I would end up in bed with a woman who was taking my clothes off. And I would think to myself, 'hey, I think this woman is into me.'"

Lea nodded knowingly and started undoing the buttons of Tori's pajama top. "You mean like this?"

Tori looked down. "Huh. That's very interesting."

"Mm-hmm. Starting to get an idea?" She bent down and kissed

Tori's chest. She ran her tongue up to Tori's neck, then her ear. "Victoria?"

"Yes?" Tori murmured. Her hands were resting on Lea's haunches, slowly moving in broad circles.

"I like you very much and I would like to have some sex with you right now." She nipped at the earlobe. "Is that a clear enough message for you?"

Tori tightened her grip on Lea's ass. "You're lucky I don't mind you teasing me."

"Because there is *so much* to tease about!" Lea laughed. She lifted up and kissed Tori's lips, dropping her voice to a seductive purr. "And because I look forward to you punishing me for it."

They kissed again and Tori swatted Lea's ass. Lea yelped and giggled into the kiss, continuing to undo the buttons until Tori's chest was exposed to her. Tori lifted her shoulders to shrug out of the top and put her hands on Lea's head as she moved down, kissing until she could close her lips around Tori's nipple. She sucked and Tori arched her back, curled her fingers in Lea's hair. She bit her lip and squirmed under the blankets. Her feet kicked the blanket away to give Lea better and easier access.

Lea sat up and moved her hands down. She hooked her thumbs in Tori's shorts and dragged them down her long legs. She tossed them toward the hamper and slid her hands down the inside of Tori's thighs, easing them apart. Her hair had fallen forward across her face, blocking one eye.

"This is what she wanted to do," Lea said.

"What?"

Lea bit her lip and leaned down. "Janice." She kissed one of Tori's thighs. "That fancy table, with the candles." She kissed the other thigh. "Free dinner. And you had to notice how dressed-up she was. She looked absolutely stunning."

Tori was breathing hard. She had one hand on her stomach, and she reached to stroke Lea's face with the other.

"She was the second-most beautiful woman there."

Lea turned her head and kissed Tori's palm. "Would you have taken her home? If we weren't together?"

Tori chuckled nervously. "That's... I don't know. Do we have to talk about this?"

"It's fine if your answer is yes," Lea said. "It's not a trap. It's not a test. I actually really liked it. Seeing a beautiful woman who wanted you. It makes me remember not to take you for granted. To appreciate how lucky I am to be with you." She ducked her head down and flicked her tongue against Tori's clit.

Tori hissed and arched her back. "Yes."

"Yes?"

"I would have gone home with her."

Lea smiled and wet her bottom lip. Then, keeping her eyes on Tori's face, she brushed her mouth against Tori's folds. She lay flat on her stomach and put her hand under Tori's ass. She reached out with her other hand, finding Tori's, linking their fingers together.

"Would you have fucked her?"

"Yes." Tori's eyes were closed. She squeezed Lea's hand. "She was gorgeous."

"Mm-hmm," Lea said, teasing and licking. "And she wanted you so bad."

Tori groaned. "Lea..."

"Victoria," she sighed, breathing across Tori's sex. She used the tip of her tongue, then the flat center, and Tori tensed to press down against her.

Lea whispered encouragement in Spanish, moved her tongue in a series of quick waves that made Tori twist and writhe under her until she came with a sharp cry that she tried to cut off at the last second. It made her sound like she was choking, and Lea chuckled as she lifted her head and kissed the soft spot just above Tori's mound.

"Do you need a drink of water, baby?"

"I need you," Tori said, grabbing the straps of Lea's tank top.

Lea pulled the shirt off and climbed up her wife's body. They kissed, Tori pushed Lea until they were both lying on their sides facing each other. Tori put her hand over Lea's mouth and Lea sucked the fingers inside. She licked and wetted them with her tongue until Tori pulled her hand free and slipped it between their bodies.

"I want you, too," Lea said quietly, bending her knee and angling her lower body toward Tori's searching hand. "Can I have you, Victoria?"

"Yes, baby." Tori slipped her hand into Lea's pajama pants, found her pussy, and pressed two fingers against her.

Lea's eyes widened, then drifted shut, and she began to move her hips. She put her hand on Tori's chest, her fingers curled, and bit her bottom lip as Tori eased a second finger inside her.

"Look at me, baby," Tori whispered.

Lea opened her eyes, whimpered, and leaned in for a kiss. "I love you."

"I love you, too." Tori pressed the heel of her hand against Lea. "Come for me, *querida*."

"Oh God..."

Tori smiled. She only knew a handful of Spanish words and phrases, but she wielded them well. She watched as Lea's face twisted, a line appearing between her eyebrows and her bottom lip trembling. Then the sharp intake of breath, the fingernails scratching Tori's shoulder, and the arched back indicating she was close.

"*Te amo*," Tori said. "I love you, Lea..."

"*Te amo*," Lea echoed as she came, brushing her lips against Tori's.

Afterward, breathing heavily with their foreheads touching, Tori kept her palm on Lea's stomach. Her fingers were still under the elastic of Lea's pants. She stroked the unseen skin with her fingertips. Lea made contented sounds in response but kept her eyes closed.

"Are you really not jealous?"

Lea peeked one eye open. "No. I won't be mad at someone for thinking you're sexy. And I won't be mad at you for having eyes." She pecked the tip of Tori's nose. "I thought she was beautiful, too."

"So you would have gone home with her, too."

"She didn't ask me," Lea said, closing her eyes again.

"I think she would have. I think if she'd seen you first, she would have."

Lea giggled quietly. The smile gave her dimples, heightened her levels of adorableness. "You are very sweet. Yes, Victoria. If she had asked me before I met you, I would definitely have gone home with her. I would have let her fuck me."

Tori didn't know why hearing that made her shiver. Maybe it was Lea's sleepy, post-orgasm voice, which could make a shopping list sound like erotica. Maybe it was just the reciprocation of Tori's own confession.

Or maybe it was something else.

She could tell Lea was already drifting off to sleep. She knew that if she held onto this thought until morning, she would lose her nerve and never bring it up. She lifted her head and kissed Lea's cheek, then moved to press her lips to the shell of Lea's ear.

"What if she wanted both of us?"

Lea inhaled sharply.

They decided to wait until morning to actually have the conversation Tori brought up. She was grateful for the chance to sleep on it, for the extra time to consider if she really meant what she'd said. Maybe it was just a dumb idea she had in the afterglow. A lot of things sounded good immediately after coming. In the shower, she cupped her hands under the water and splashed it into her face, ran her fingers through her hair.

Janice was gorgeous. And if Lea was right, and the invitation was supposed to be a date, it meant she was attracted to Tori. And anyone would be attracted to Lea. Beautiful, talented, funny, ray of sunshine Lea.

She didn't know how she would feel seeing Lea with someone else. Even if they agreed on ground rules ahead of time, it felt scary. She didn't think Lea would fall for Janice. Of course she barely knew Janice, and there was a chance *she* would become obsessed with one of them. She couldn't imagine someone sleeping with Lea and not falling completely in love. But Janice had completely shifted gears when she found out Tori wasn't available. She was confident if they were clear and upfront about what it would be, there wasn't much danger in going through with it. They didn't really need a boost in the bedroom, their sex life was fantastic. But there didn't seem to be any harm in exploring. Having a little fun.

When she got out of the shower, she found Lea cooking breakfast. She was wearing one of Tori's fire department T-shirts which was long enough to serve as a dress on her.

"How dare you wear my clothes, take that off right now."

Lea laughed and plucked at the hem. "I'm making *huevos rotos*. Pour me some orange juice and I'll serve you."

"That sounds like a deal." Tori got the jug from the fridge. "So... did you think more about last night?"

"Mm, yes, perhaps," Lea said, throwing a sultry look over her shoulder. "And perhaps I'll think about it in the shower in a while."

Tori grinned. "No, I meant... about the thing. What I said after."

Lea stopped stirring the eggs and potatoes. "Wait, were you being serious?"

"Yeah." Tori returned the juice to the fridge. "I mean... yeah. Obviously the answer can be no. But I think it's worth thinking about."

"I guess you have a point." Lea was staring at the backsplash behind the stove, her spatula hanging forgotten above the pan.

Tori stepped closer and guided Lea's hand down. Lea looked down, realized she'd gotten distracted, and resumed cooking.

"Discussing it doesn't mean *doing* it," Tori said again. "But when we were talking about it while you were going down on me, it... it definitely... heightened things. If it's something we want to actually explore, we probably won't get a more perfect opportunity than we have right now."

"That's true." Lea sighed and cocked her hip. "I've never actually considered a threesome. Not, like, in real life. That's not something people really do, right?"

"It happens," Tori said. "It usually doesn't live up to the fantasy, from what I hear, but it's not a fictional occurrence."

"Hm." She lifted the spatula and bit the flat end, her eyes staring through the wall again.

Tori said, "Babe, biting the cookware is not sanitary."

"Oh, please," Lea scolded. "Go sit down, let me serve you."

"Yes, ma'am."

They shifted to the kitchen table, where Lea served the breakfast and took a seat across from Tori.

"So if we did do it, the other person would be... it would be Janice? Right?"

"Is there someone else you think~"

"No, no," Lea said quickly, shaking her head. "She likes you, I think she's sexy, so it makes sense, as long as she finds *me* attractive."

Tori leaned to the side and scanned Lea's body under the table. "I think that's a safe bet."

Lea blushed. "Okay. So, yes. It makes sense it would be her. But... what if we ask her and she says no? What if she's not into it for whatever reason? Do we... keep looking for someone else?" She took a bite of her eggs. "I guess what I'm asking, are we deciding to have a threesome, or are we deciding to have a threesome with Janice? And if she says no, we don't do it."

"Huh." Tori leaned back. "I hadn't thought about that. I just assumed she would jump at the chance."

Lea arched an eyebrow. "Egotistical."

"Hey, you're the one who said she wanted to jump me. I'm just working off your hypothesis."

Lea giggled, and it was such a beautiful sound that Tori was almost distracted from their conversation.

"I don't think I'd want to do it with some random person," Tori decided. "I know Janice is basically a random person. We've met twice."

"I've only met her once."

"Well, you're meeting her this weekend when I'm at work, so we'll be even then. But since she's the whole reason we're talking about this, it seems like it should be her or no one."

Lea nodded. "I agree. The idea of trying to find someone…" She shook her head and cut her hand through the air. "No, no. If Janice says no, we'll just drop it."

"That works for me." Tori took a few bites of her breakfast before she spoke again. "Of course this is the easy part. Deciding we're interested in doing it. The tough part will be bringing it up to Janice."

Lea shrugged. "I will go up to her when we meet this weekend, and I will say, 'Hello, Janice, I can't wait to spend the day with you, by the way, do you want to have sex with me and my wife?' What's so tough about that?"

Tori said, "You're a brat."

"Mm-hmm," Lea said, chipperly. "But truthfully, I will have the whole day with her. I can feel her out and see if I think she'd be receptive to it."

"I trust you to come up with something casual."

When they finished their breakfast, Tori got up and cleared her plate. She came back into the kitchen and bent down to kiss Lea goodbye.

"See you tomorrow, love," Lea said, brushing her fingers down Tori's jaw. "Be safe."

"Always. I love you."

"I love you, too."

She grabbed her bag on her way out the door. Part of her regretted bringing up such a huge subject moments before leaving for a full-day shift, but it also seemed good they would both have a chance to think about it on their own. It wasn't the sort of thing you could think about with someone breathing down her neck

It wasn't until she arrived at work that she realized the firehouse probably wasn't the best place for deep thinking. Conrad Weaver and Annie Vest were in the lounge playing a video game, shouting at the screen or at each other, while Freddy Carpenter was in the kitchen preparing lunch. Freddy was their probationary officer and, as such, was forced to do the jobs that no one else wanted to do. This particular chore worked out well for everyone, because he liked cooking and everyone loved his food.

Tori paused on her way to the locker room to sneak a peek at what he was preparing. He blocked the pot with his shoulder.

"You'll find out with everyone else, nosy parker. Just keep moving along."

"Rude," she said. "I thought you were supposed to respect your elders."

"There are so many elders around here, I'm taking it on a case-by-case basis."

Tori laughed and dropped her things off in the locker. By the time she got back to the lounge, Annie had emerged victorious in the fighting game.

"It's about time you showed up," Conrad said. "I need to play with someone I can actually beat."

"Sorry, Con." Tori sat down on the couch under the window and put her feet up. "Some of us have wives who make breakfast for us, and that can make us late."

Conrad shook his head. "Sounds like hell. I just grab a McMuffin on the way to work and I'm on time, every time, like a good boy."

Annie said, "And we're all very impressed." She put down her controller and turned her recliner around. She raised her eyebrows at Tori and smiled. "Lea still spoiling you?"

"Every day and sometimes twice a night," Tori said, an old joke from when they first started dating. "I forget what she called breakfast. It was some kind of eggs and potatoes thing. Absolutely divine."

"I hate you," Annie groaned. "Gorgeous wife *and* she cooks for you. It's so unfair!"

Tori took out her phone. She glanced at Conrad, who was playing a solo version of his game. She pointed at her phone, then at Annie's, and started typing a text. "Have you ever had a 3some?"

Annie's phone chimed and she looked down. She arched an eyebrow and slowly looked back up at Tori. Tori typed a follow-up.

"NOT an invitation." After a second, she added, "No offense."

Annie chuckled and looked over her shoulder at Conrad. She stood and motioned with her head for Tori to follow her.

They went into the apparatus bay and Annie did a quick check to make sure they were alone.

"First of all, I was flattered but I would've said no because we work together."

"That's fair," Tori said.

Annie crossed her arms. "So if it wasn't the most blunt invitation of all time, what was it?"

Tori sighed and sat on the bumper of the engine. "Do you remember the nothing call at Canvas? The kitchen fire?"

"Vaguely, yeah. The owner was hitting on you."

"Oh for crying out loud." Tori rolled her eyes as she slumped in defeat. "Did everyone see it?"

Annie shook her head. "No. No, not everyone. Chief was back here at the station, so he missed it. David filled him in, though."

"Great," Tori muttered. "Well, it turns out you're all right. Janice *was* hitting on me. So when I showed up to dinner last night with my wife, it was... well, let's just say she was disappointed."

"What did Lea say?"

"She thought it was hilarious I didn't know. And then we talked about it a little more, and I sort of brought up the idea of maybe... possibly..."

Annie laughed. "Wow! Wow. So what did Lea say to *that?*"

"I think she's into it. But I don't know. Now I'm worried if she goes along with it, it will just be because she thinks it's what I want."

"And you don't know if you want."

"Right. I don't *not* want. Janice is a very beautiful woman." She held her hands up helplessly. "But I don't know what it would be like in the moment. And it's not like you can get right up to the moment and say 'time out, I changed my mind.'"

"Of course you can," Annie said. "And anyone who doesn't agree isn't worth doing it with in the first place." She walked over and sat next to Tori on the bumper. "Look, it doesn't have to be all-in, all at once. You can test the waters a little bit. Have another dinner. Get to know her a little bit. Gradual. Like any other person you're thinking of taking to bed. The only difference this time is that your wife will be there, too."

Tori raised an eyebrow. "That helps, actually. Just treat it like any other date. Thanks for talking me through it."

"Sure. Glad I could help you get laid while I'm still horribly single." She patted Tori's leg and stood up.

"Hey, you never answered the original question."

Annie stopped on her way to the door. "Yeah, once."

"Was it worth all the hassle?"

"Nah," Annie said. "But don't go by my experience. It all depends on the people involved. Get the right people, you never know what might happen." She headed for the door again. "Considering you and Lea are involved, I'd say you're already off to a pretty good start."

When she was gone, Tori chewed her lip and thought about what she'd said. She also thought about what Freddy said about respecting his elders.

"Case-by-case basis. Could work..."

Chapter Four

LEA ROLLED over and looked at the empty bed next to her. After six years together and three years of marriage, she still couldn't get used to how many nights she spent alone. That was supposed to be one of the best perks, right? No more lonely nights in a big bed. Tori had been home all day Friday, but she left at midnight and wouldn't be back until Sunday morning. That was what she'd signed up for. And the first few months, it had been great. All the perks of being in a relationship with built-in absences so she could do her own thing.

Now, though...

She didn't feel neglected. Nothing of the sort. Tori was present when she was home, and she was always available for a phone call or texting. It wasn't like she was alone or dealing with a long distance relationship. Tori was just a few miles down the road. She could run home if necessary, get someone to cover her shift in an emergency. But Lea was not going to make her loneliness anyone else's problem. She could deal with a few solitary mornings.

She sat up and stretched her arms over her head before throwing back the blankets. Today was going to be anything but lonely. She and Janice had arranged to meet by Buckingham Fountain at noon. It would be full of tourists, but it was a good place to start. The fountain itself was one of the cliché sights she hoped to avoid, but there were small statues of children nearby that most tourists ignored. Dove Girl, Turtle Boy, Fisher Boy, and Crane Girl. They were lovely, and thought they deserved to be honored.

Lea mentally planned their excursion while she was in the shower. She was excited to be Janice's guide. She had started to take Chicago for granted. She just saw the trash on the L, only paid attention to the architecture when she was looking for a place to take shelter from the wind. She couldn't wait to see it through someone else's eyes, to remember why she'd fallen in love with the city in the first place.

Before she left, she sent Tori a message letting her know their plan was underway. She waited until she was on the train before she texted Janice. "I'll be in a big red coat."

"Shouldn't be too hard to spot," Janice sent back quickly. "On my way, too. Blue peacoat, big black gloves, white knit cap."

Lea arrived first as she expected. It was too late in the season for the fountain to be running, but tourists had still shown up. She stood well away from the crowd and brought her camera up, watching everyone move through the viewfinder. She saw what looked like a reunion - loud laughter, big crushing hug - and snapped a photo. She had more film in her bag if she needed it, and she'd also brought a digital camera just in case. She didn't have to worry about wasting a shot. She was always grateful for a perfect candid moment like that. She was wandering through the pavilion when she caught a glimpse of a white knit cap moving through the crowd. She moved to intercept.

Janice spotted her and grinned. She lifted her hand in a wave and walked toward her. They met in the middle. Lea wasn't sure if this meeting required a handshake, definitely not a hug, or just the awkward 'hi, hello' they exchanged. Janice kept the smile on her face as she turned and looked at the fountain.

"Wow. This is beautiful."

"It is. You should see it running in all its glory. But the design is still worth admiring. And it definitely says *Chicago* in a big loud voice."

Janice nodded. "So I should avoid things like this..."

"No, no, not necessarily. You should definitely have the classics, the defining sights. There's nothing wrong with a picture of an L train or the Bean. But you don't want it to be your centerpiece."

"Makes sense," Janice said.

Lea held up her camera. "I'll get a few shots, just in case. You can decide when we have more pictures and you have more of an idea of your options."

"Excellent."

Lea took pictures from a handful of angles. It was impossible to find a shot without tourists in it, but she tried her best to only get the backs of their heads. If push came to shove, she could blur or obscure any faces that made it into a shot they used. Janice followed her as she changed positions, staying close but never crowding her or trying to peek at the viewfinder. Lea appreciated that and, as a reward, frequently stopped to show her a picture she'd taken.

"Even if we don't use these for the restaurant," Janice said, "they're still gorgeous."

Lea beamed. "That's the beauty of photography. You don't have to know what or who the pictures are for. Sometimes they are just pretty."

"That can be more than enough."

"Mm-hmm!" Lea agreed. "Now, come with me. There are some statues I want to show you. Are you okay with walking? There's another place I want to show you, but we have to walk a little."

Janice nodded and gestured at Lea. "I'll follow where you go."

"Then we should get along just fine! And we're walking. This way."

The Fountain Figures statues stood in their own reflecting ponds flanking the main fountain, two north and two south. For the next few minutes, Lea took photos and showed them to Janice, who gave suggestions for different angles. The statues were situated inside a rose garden, which was unfortunately not as eye-catching in the winter.

"We can come back when everything has bloomed. It's so beautiful. They have orange roses! I had never seen anything like them before. And then you could have seasonal artwork. Keeping things fresh and new."

"That's a lot of work for you," Janice said.

"Oh, I don't mind."

Janice said, "Yeah, but this is work for you. I feel like I'm taking advantage."

"You gave us a free meal, so this is returning the favor. Any future work will be professional rates. Like when Tori and I go back to Canvas. Deal?"

Janice smiled. "Definitely a deal."

Lea grinned at her and gestured to the path out of the garden. "This way now. We have to walk a block or two, but it's really going to be worth the effort."

"I look forward to it."

Lea led her down the sidewalk, sticking close to her side. Once they had crossed Michigan Avenue, she thought about her side project for the day. At some point she was supposed to casually bring up the idea of having a threesome with this woman. She remembered being a bit flirtatious back when she was single, and she knew that she and Tori would never have gotten together if she hadn't taken the initiative. But six years was a long time. She felt rusty. She didn't even know how to broach the subject.

"So." She winced. "Uh. H-have you lived in Chicago long?"

"About a year," Janice said. "Originally from Seattle. Then the pandemic hit, lost my job, lost my girlfriend, and I decided if I was going to stuff my savings into a bottomless pit, I might as well take a leap and try to make it worthwhile. Chicago made more sense financially, so I headed out here to see if I could make my restaurant dream come true."

"Looks like you're making a pretty good go of it."

Janice shrugged. "It's still early days. Savings definitely took a hit, but I think I can see the light at the end of the tunnel."

"Good, good. I'm sorry about losing your job and your girlfriend, though. That sounds rough."

"It was, at the time," Janice said. "But honestly, if we couldn't survive being locked up together for a few weeks, it wasn't going to last anyway. *C'est la vie*, right?"

Lea nodded. "That's a good way of looking at it." She held out her arm to indicate a turn. "Right here. This is the Wabash Arts Corridor. The businesses have an arrangement with Columbia College to use their blank walls for murals. We're going to see my favorites right now. Luckily they're right next to each other."

"Oh, I can't wait."

They had to pass under the L tracks to reach it, and Janice asked Lea to stop and take a few shots of the framework.

"Sorry if that's dorky," she said as Lea complied, tilting her head back to look up at the girders. "But I've always loved them. They're definitely iconic Chicago."

"They are." Lea showed her the pictures she had taken. "We can hang around until a train goes by, get a few action shots."

"Oh, that would look cool. Okay. Thank you for indulging me.

Onward to the art!"

They stepped out from under the tracks into a parking lot. Lea gestured at the wall like a magician revealing the end of a trick. Janice actually gasped when she saw it. There were two pieces of artwork painted on the building. The main draw was a six-story mural which featured a little girl at the bottom holding open a book. The air above her was full of fluttering pages from the book, each one featuring a different historic woman. The space between the portraits was occupied by soaring blue sparrows.

"Oh wow!" Janice said softly. "How did I not notice this. You even told me the art would be up on a wall. But this is amazing."

"Isn't it? I just love it. It was painted by an artist named Jasmina Cazacu."

Janice moved closer. "I recognize Ida B. Wells. We were just on the street named for her. But I'm afraid I'd embarrass myself if I tried to name anyone else."

"I can't name them all off the top of my head, either," Lea admitted. "But there's Ida Wells, Myra Blackwell, Grace Wilbur Trout..." There were ten in all, and she was ashamed she couldn't list more. "You can add a list of their names to the display. Your restaurant will be beautiful art *and* educational."

"That's everyone's dream, right?" Janice laughed. "But no, this will look amazing. I already know exactly where I want to put it. How big are the prints going to be?"

Lea shrugged. "As big or small as you want. We can get measurements once we know what will be going where." She smiled and pointed at the painting that shared the wall with the suffragettes. "Now, it's probably not politically correct to say I favor this over the powerful women from history. But..."

Janice laughed. "It's very striking."

It was a giant picture of a moose blowing a big pink bubble of chewing gum.

"The blue background really makes the whole thing pop," Lea sad. "No pun intended. You know. Bubble gum, pop."

"Right," Janice said. "It might be less important, but art is art. And this..." She jabbed a finger at the moose. "This is amazing art."

"I have to agree."

Lea took a couple of pictures of the murals, then stepped back. "Why don't you get in one?"

"Me? I'm not going to hang a picture of myself in my restaurant."

Lea said, "No, but for yourself. You can use it on the website, or social media, or whatever. Let people know that the owner of Canvas can appreciate the culture of Chicago."

Janice laughed, shrugged, and stepped forward. She held her arms out to frame the moose. Lea snapped a photo.

"Beautiful!" she said. "Show me passion! Show me fierce!"

Janice cocked her hip to the side and twisted her lips into a snarl. Lea laughed.

"Perfect!"

She was still taking photos when her phone chimed in her pocket. She apologized and pulled it out, saw Tori's face smiling back at her, and juggled her camera so she could answer.

"It's Tori."

"Oh, go ahead," Janice said.

Lea swept the screen. "Hi, *querida*..."

"Hi," Tori said, speaking quickly and quietly. Lea imagined she was in the bunkroom where she wouldn't be overheard. "Listen, are you with Janice?"

"I am. Wh~"

"Did you talk to her about it yet?"

"Uh." Lea glanced at Janice, who was examining the suffragette mural. "No, not yet."

Tori sighed in relief. "Okay. Good. Don't."

Lea blinked in surprise. She started to speak, stopped herself, then put the phone against her shoulder. "Janice, do you speak Spanish?"

"No."

"Okay. Then I am about to be very rude, and I apologize." She brought the phone back up and switched to Spanish. "What are you talking about? Did you change your mind? I understand if you did, but this is cutting it a little close."

"No," Tori said in English. "I didn't change my mind. Not about what we decided on. But I was thinking about bringing it up this way. It's a terrible way to go about it. We need to be together so she knows without a doubt where we both stand. Otherwise it just looks like you're hitting on her."

Lea said, "I don't think she would make that leap."

"I didn't either. But then I obsessed on it, and it festered in my head. I'm not saying the worst-case scenario will happen. I'm just saying that asking her when we're together is the right way to do it."

"I can agree with that. It takes some pressure off of me, too. I was a little anxious."

"Yeah, I know. I'm sorry I put it all on you, baby."

Lea smiled, grateful for the apology she didn't realize she wanted. "You're forgiven. You can make it up to me somehow."

"I'll figure something out. In the meantime, invite her to our place for dinner tomorrow night. We can talk about it then."

"Okay. Love you."

"I love you," Tori said.

When Lea hung up, Janice stopped pretending to study the mural. "I hope everything is okay."

"Oh, fine fine," Lea said, waving at the phone like it was inconsequential. "Just couple stuff. But it reminded me. Um. Tori, um, wanted me to invite you over to our place for dinner some night. Tomorrow. Tomorrow night."

Janice raised her eyebrows. "Oh!"

"If you're free," Lea added quickly. "I know it's very short notice. It's just that with her schedule, it's a little hard to work out when~"

"No, tomorrow's fine. The restaurant can handle itself for one night. I would love that." She tucked her hair behind her ear, smiling. "You know, since moving here, I've spent so much time trying to get Canvas off the ground and then keeping it afloat, I haven't had much chance to socialize. It would be really great to have some friends around."

"Right!" Lea said. "Everyone needs local friends. And this wouldn't be repayment or a favor or anything. No strings attached, just like friends."

"Just like friends," Janice agreed, chuckling.

Lea cleared her throat and lifted the camera again. "Now, if you're ready, we have eight more blocks of murals to investigate. Are you up for it?"

Janice flexed her arm and nodded. "Let's go!"

Lea giggled and ducked her chin, marching out of the parking lot with Janice in tow. She hadn't realized how heavily the threesome invite had been weighing on her. Now that it had been lifted, so felt like she could let loose and enjoy the afternoon for what it was. Just two new friends running around downtown, looking at art. The only way it could be improved was if Tori could have been there with them. But, as it stood, it was already shaping up to be a pretty great day.

Two hours later, they slowly made their way back to Grant Park, where they'd left their cars. They had taken a plethora of potential photos for Canvas, and Lea had convinced Janice to pose for a few more "for advertising." She only agreed if Lea let herself be the subject of a few photos. It was a fight to make her give up her camera, but she eventually relented and got into the spirit of playing tourist in her own town.

They were nearly to the parking garage when a siren suddenly whooped into existence. Lea stopped in her tracks at the first wail, whipping her head toward the origin. Her breath was caught in her throat as her eyes scanned the buildings and tried to pinpoint which street the truck was on, which direction it was going. She let her breath out only when she had that information, relaxing enough to search the area for smoke.

"Everything okay?" Janice asked.

"Oh." Lea laughed. She put her hand on her forehead, suddenly embarrassed. She had forgotten the other woman was there for a second. "Yes, I'm sorry. Every time I hear a fire truck siren, I panic. Even if I'm nowhere near Tori's station, like now."

Janice nodded. "No, I absolutely get it. That makes sense."

Lea started walking again. "Some people claim you can't tell the difference between fire trucks and police or ambulances or whatever. I didn't think so, either." She held up a finger. "But there is a difference. Even before the fire truck has to be honking its horn at the *gilipollas* who don't get out of the damned way."

"I would probably do the same thing," Janice admitted. "It must be nerve-wracking to have a partner in such a dangerous profession."

"Mm," Lea said. "It actually sort of helps that there's nothing to be done about it. I would never ask her to change her job. And she is a very good firefighter, but it wouldn't matter if she was the best. Fires don't care how good she is. I cannot protect her so I learn to live with the possibility. And that means sometimes I get a little jumpy."

"I'm sure Tori appreciates it."

Lea looked up sharply. "Oh, I don't tell her. No. She knows I worry, of course. But she would feel awful if she knew how high I jumped every time I hear a siren. I feel like telling her would just make her guilty over something she has no control over."

"Maybe it's something you could work through together."

"Maybe." Lea shrugged.

They had arrived at the garage where Janice had parked, and Lea revealed her car was a little further south. Janice opened her arms for a hug, which Lea eagerly gave.

"I had a wonderful time today," Lea said.

"Me too. I can't wait to see the pictures."

"I'm sure they came out beautifully. I'll have some ready for you to look at tomorrow night."

"And I'll get some measurements of the restaurant."

Lea snapped her fingers. "*Perfecta.* I will text you with the address. Seven?"

"I think that works for me, but I'll confirm. I can't wait."

"Me neither. Be safe, Janice."

"You too, Lea."

She watched Janice walk into the garage, waiting until she turned a corner out of sight before she started walking herself.

Whatever happened at dinner tomorrow, she was confident that she and Tori would at least end up with a very good friend. And if that was the worst-case scenario, she couldn't wait to see how the chips fell.

CHAPTER FIVE

CONRAD MANAGED to hold off for almost the entire call. But as they were walking out, he turned and held out his arms as if addressing a crowd. "Ladies and gentlemen... Arcade Fire!"

Tori rolled her eyes. "Seriously, Con? These people could have lost their business."

"Yeah, but they didn't. It's fine." He dropped his arms and looked around the arcade. "A little paint, some rewiring, it will be good as new."

"You know it's not that simple. Once they deal with all the damage, replacing the machines that were totaled, and pay to clean up all the smoke and water damage, they could be deeply in debt. It's not the time to make jokes."

"All right, all right."

Tori climbed into the truck where Annie was already strapped in. David went around the front and got behind the wheel. The owners actually hadn't even been there to hear his comment, but he'd been getting far too comfortable with 'jokes' like that lately. It was best to nip it in the bud as much as possible before he said something at the wrong time and caused real problems.

Once they were on the road, Annie nudged Tori's foot with hers. "Did you see they had Mega Man 2?"

David said, "Oh yeah! I ruled that game in high school."

"They had video games way back then?" He flipped her off. Tori grinned. "I was more of a pinball gal."

"They had a couple of those, too," Annie said. "Once they're back up and running, I might go back and spend a few quarters."

"Sounds like an expensive reminder of how long ago high school was," Tori said.

Annie laughed. "Rude. True. But rude." She looked into the cab, where Conrad and Freddy were talking about some movie one of them had seen that weekend. She leaned closer to Tori's seat and lowered her voice. "So the thing you and Lea were talking about...?"

"Uh yeah." Tori cleared her throat. She watched the guys to make sure neither of them became interested. "Yeah. She's... they're talking today. Meeting up today."

"She's *with her?*" Annie said.

Tori shushed her. "Yeah. Doing some photography. We're going to have dinner together and we'll talk it out then."

"Wow. That's... wow. I mean, hey, good luck. Let me know if I'm prying too much, because this is... you know... private. But I'm just so intrigued by the whole thing." She held out her fist. "I'm rooting for you."

Tori chuckled and tapped her knuckles against Annie's. "I'll tell you the PG version."

"Works for me."

When they got back to the station, Tori volunteered to clean the rig. It was an easy way to earn a favor from the others and also bought her some time to herself. She had spent the entire day thinking about Lea and Janice together. She kept wondering where they were, what they were doing, what they might be talking about. It had helped out in the end, since her obsessing made her realize their tactical error, but she knew she needed to drop it.

It wasn't like they were on a date. But it was definitely *like* they were on a *date*. Lea was absolutely irresistible when she got talking about photography. They were going to see the fountain and statues, and they would definitely head down the Wabash Arts Corridor. And Tori could help but see the parallels between this and the day she met Lea. If she could fall in love with Lea by walking around the block with her, how could Janice resist after a whole afternoon?

She wanted to call and see how things were going. But she knew that was the wrong choice. She checked her watch. Maybe they were done. Maybe Lea was dying to talk about it. No. If that was the case, Lea would call her. Lea probably needed time to process everything that had been said before Tori started bombarding her with questions.

But she was dying to know what had been said.

And she hated the idea that Lea would spend the whole day with this other woman, this virtual stranger to them both, and then go to bed alone. She wondered how Lea would bring up the topic. It had to be awkward to just *say* Tori was on board with it and just expect Janice to believe her. In fact, the more Tori thought about it, the more she thought it would sound like a lie. Cheaters who claimed they were in open relationships, while their spouse was blissfully unaware of that status.

Her mind rolled around that thought until it was so big she couldn't think of anything else. She finally decided that they had to tell Janice together, otherwise it ran the risk of sounding sketchy. She went outside where she could be guaranteed privacy and called Lea to put the kibosh on any invitations. Tori could hear the relief in her voice when she agreed to the change in plans.

She sighed, relieved that they had avoided a potentially fatal mistake. She nearly ran into the captain on her way back to the apparatus bay. David glanced at her but didn't slow down as he passed.

"Going for a walk, Branigan?" he said over his shoulder. "Shirkin' your workin'?"

"Hey, I just cleaned the whole damn rig," she said. "What have *you* done today?"

He cackled and flipped her off without looking back.

She spent the rest of the day doing busywork around the station. She cleaned the apparatus bay, did inventory, helped Freddy with dinner, and even volunteered to wash the dishes afterward. She kept herself so preoccupied that Gambol actually came up to her as she was putting away the last of the plates.

"You know I was just teasing you about–"

"Yeah," she said.

He nodded. "Okay, just making sure. So... are you okay? You always run like you're set to eleven, but right now you're closer to twenty."

She said, "I've just got a lot on my mind. Trying to push it out."

"Fair enough. Let me know if you ever need to talk."

"Thanks, Cap."

They ended the day by watching a movie in the lounge, something actiony with Daniel Craig, so Tori was successfully able to turn off her brain and stare at the screen. It was almost midnight by the time she headed for her bunk. Annie was already asleep, so Tori kept the light off as she changed into her night clothes - sweatpants and a tank top that could easily be covered by her gear if she got a call - and sat on the edge of her bed.

She started to call, then decided a text would be easier to pass off as casual. Plus it wouldn't disturb Annie's sleep. She turned down the brightness of her screen and switched to silent. She felt like a teenager trying to text her girlfriend without being caught by her parents.

"How'd everything go today?" She chewed her lip and stared at the screen, waiting for three dots to appear. She had just started to put the phone down when a reply popped up.

"I was just thinking about you." With a kissing emoji. A second text followed, answering her. "Fantastic! I really like her. She's funny. She likes the same kind of art as me, so of course we bonded." A big laugh emoji, then a second text. "Seriously though she's great."

Tori felt unexpectedly smacked by the message. Her thumb trembled above the keypad, tempted to type out that she wouldn't stand in their way and she hoped they would be very happy together. Before the demons could succeed in pulling her down the dark path, more messages showed up. Pictures, samples from the day Lea and Janice had spent together.

Tori couldn't help but smile when she saw the photos. She clicked on one, a selfie angled up to catch the L passing above her. Janice was also in the picture, leaning into frame and doing what Lea called 'big teeth smiling.' Tori pinched the image to enlarge Lea's smiling face. The tremor in her thumb went away, and she felt the tension between her shoulders evaporate.

"Gorgeous work as always, baby. You have such a great eye. And great eyes."

"Flirt," Lea immediately sent back. "I got a lot of really good pictures. It was a good day."

"I'm glad. I can't wait to see all your beautiful art."

"I can't wait to see YOU. I miss you."

Tori exhaled and tapped her fingers on the back of her phone. "I miss you too. But you should be asleep. You had a big day."

"You're the one who texted me!" Tongue sticking out emoji.

"Tell me what did you do today?"

"Electrical fire. Nothing major. We watched a movie. Daniel Craig."

"Bond. James Bond."

"I don't think so. I wasn't paying attention. There was an actress that looked like you."

"Oh yeah?"

"She kicked a lot of ass."

A laughing emoji. "Well, of course she did!" A pause, and then a screenshot of Daniel Craig and an actress in a black evening dress. "Was it this?"

"That's the one."

"That's Bond."

Tori grinned. It was definitely the right actors, but they hadn't worn anything near that fancy in the movie she'd seen. "If you say so. What did you do all night?"

"Prep on dinner for tomorrow. Worked on the photos. Some really gorgeous ones. But now..."

The next message was a photo of Lea with her head on the pillow, lips pursed in a kiss. Tori smiled and laid down, snapped a duplicate picture, and sent it in response.

"Beautiful," Lea sent back.

"I'm glad you think so," Tori typed. "You're wearing the pajamas I got you."

"Yes, I love them. They're very cozy."

Tori glanced over her shoulder. Annie was still fast asleep, facing the wall. Tori bit her bottom lip and looked at the screen again.

"You should take them off."

"lol but you can't do anything."

"So do it for me."

There was a long pause. Then: "Chilly."

"I wish I could warm you up."

"(making happy noises)"

"I love your happy noises."

Lea sent a winking emoji. "You can hear them tomorrow."

"Tomorrow. Can't wait."

"ILU."

"ILU2," Tori sent back.

Tori turned off the phone and placed it facedown on the nightstand. She felt ten pounds lighter, mentally and physically. She lay on her back, hands laced together on her stomach. She was still entirely onboard with talking to Janice and whatever happened afterward. She'd never realistically entertained the idea of a threesome, but now that they were standing on the threshold, she had to admit she was excited. But at the same time she couldn't quite fathom the reality of it.

How could she possibly be okay with sharing Lea with anyone, even if it was just for one night?

She fell asleep contemplating the question, which prevented her from answering it.

Tori's shift ended with a hotel room fire at three in the morning. Tori was the first through the door, pausing in the vestibule to check the fire alarm control panel mounted by the door. Second Floor Detection was lit up, and she'd called back to the others to let them know where they were going. An employee at the foot of the stairs directed them to the back of the building. Conrad took the employee to the front desk to confirm how many guests were in the building while the rest of the team stomped their way up the stairs.

The next few hours were spent putting out a small fire started by someone who fell asleep smoking a cigarette. The fire had been contained to a single room, so there was no need to evacuate. Several guests had moved to the lobby, however, and were milling around in their pajamas when the job was finally complete.

The sun had risen while they were in the building, and the truck returned to the station so they could clock out.

Lea was still in bed when Tori got home. She was sitting up doing the crossword on her phone. Tori undressed down to her underwear, leaned across the bed to kiss Lea, then collapsed onto the mattress. Lea chuckled and put down her puzzle to rearrange Tori's limbs and tuck her in.

"Tough day?" she asked once Tori had been repositioned.

"Normal day," Tori said without opening her eyes. "But way too much of it happened right before dawn, and I barely got any sleep."

Lea left a series of featherweight kisses along Tori's eyelids and down her cheek. "Poor baby. You just stay here and rest. I'll take care of everything for tonight."

Tori said, "What's on your plate?"

"I have to go shopping to get some of the things for dinner. I'll do that while you're sleeping. Then I just have to make the meal, shower, and get dressed."

"Wake me up while you're cooking. I'll help tidy the place up."

Lea bent down and kissed Tori's lips. "I'll see you in a few hours."

"Hmm," Tori said, already drifting off.

She was aware of Lea slipping out of bed, getting dressed, and showering, but everything after that was a dreamy haze.

The next time she was fully awake, the apartment had filled with the scent of cooking meat. She climbed out of bed and let the aroma pull her into the kitchen. Lea was at the counter in jeans and a white T-shirt. She smiled at Tori.

"*Lechon asado*," Lea said.

Tori hugged her from behind and kissed her neck. "You made that for me on our first Christmas together. Happy memories."

Lea pressed back against her. "Well, however tonight goes, I wanted us all to be at least well-fed." She turned and kissed Tori's lips. "Sleep well?"

"You know I sleep better with you," Tori said, resting her hands on Lea's hips. "But decent enough."

Lea purred and then pointed toward the counter. "I got extra oranges."

Tori smiled. "Why?"

"Because I love you and think about you when you're not here." She twisted and turned in Tori's arms. She kissed her, and then pointed at the counter again. "Go get one. I'll peel it for you."

"You spoil me." Tori went to retrieve the orange and brought it back.

She passed it to Lea, their fingers brushing. Lea placed it on the counter and rolled it back and forth with her palm, then used a knife to cut a divot into the skin. While she was working, Tori put her hands on the counter and hopped up, scooting back and watching the process. Lea traded the knife for a spoon, slipping it under the rind and working it back and forth until she could peel it away and expose the fruit. When she was finished, she cut the orange in half between peeled and unpeeled.

Lea stepped into the V of Tori's legs and broke off a segment. She carefully plucked a segment free, and Tori opened her mouth. Lea placed it on her tongue, then swept her thumb across Tori's bottom lip to smear the juices there.

"Good?" Lea asked, cocking an eyebrow.

"Delicious," Tori said, holding eye contact as she licked the juices away.

Lea bit her bottom lip and readied another segment. She ran her tongue over one flat side and presented it to Tori, who caught it between her teeth.

When it was gone, she said, "Someone's a little wired."

"May-be," Lea said, drawing the word out to two syllables. "I'm excited about tonight."

Tori grinned. "You really like her, huh?"

"We talked for so long yesterday. Just walking around, looking at art, showing her the city. There's so much art in the city! And people don't know to look for it!"

Tori laughed. "I know, baby. You took me on the same tour. I'm glad she appreciated it."

"She did. We got so many pictures, gosh." She shook her head. "We could wallpaper the whole restaurant with them. I'm glad she's making the final decisions and not me." She sighed and tilted her head to the side. "Even if she's not into, you know, what we suggest, I think she could be a very good friend. So long as asking doesn't make things awkward."

Tori put her hands on Lea's hips. "We'll just have to be very clear that there's no pressure. Yes or no, either way, we're happy."

"Yes." Lea kissed Tori's lips and made a 'mm' sound when she tasted the orange on them. "Now hop down. You still need to shower and find something nice to wear."

"That's not going to take me all day."

"Find something to wear," Lea repeated.

Tori sighed and hopped off the counter. "Right. Give me my orange."

Lea handed it to her, then lightly gripped her wrist. "The shimmery maroon blouse. Black slacks. With the big belt."

"You think she'll like that?" Tori asked.

"*I* like it."

"Good enough for me." She leaned in and kissed Lea on the eyebrow. "Will you wear the strawberry dress for me?"

"Mm-hmm."

"Mm," Tori said. "Tonight's gonna be great."

CHAPTER SIX

JANICE WOKE with a smile on Sunday morning. At first she wasn't sure what had prompted it. She didn't remember having any dreams, but slowly she remembered how she had spent the day before. The entire time she'd lived in Chicago, she'd never spent an entire day just wandering around appreciating the beauty of her adopted town. There was so much art hiding around corners and in alleyways that she'd never bothered to look for.

And of course, there was Lea.

She rolled onto her back and whispered a curse under her breath. Why did Lea have to be so beautiful? And friendly? And sweet? Janice rubbed a hand over her face. It was frustrating as hell. Doubly so, since she'd been just as attracted to Tori when she first saw her. Who wouldn't? Firefighter. Uniform. Tall. Dark. Handsome, if a woman could be called that. She didn't think "pretty" was right for someone with such sharp features.

"A handsome woman," she said out loud. It sounded right, so she decided to go with it.

Then it turned out she was unavailable. Fine. Janice could deal with that disappointment. It wasn't like she'd had enough time to get attached to the fantasy before it was shattered. But to then find out that Tori's wife was just as attractive? Just as desirable? It wasn't fair. It made sense, for two people like that to meet each other and lock it down, but it was selfish of them.

She kicked away the blankets and took her phone off the charger. She scrolled back to the last texts Lea had sent her the night before. She had sent the address and directions, along with a quick rundown of what she was planning to cook.

"Any restrictions I need to know about?" Lea had asked.

"Go wild," Janice had sent back. "Wine?"

"Yes please!!"

Janice smiled again at the exuberance, which had been followed by a heart-eye emoji.

She put the phone down and twisted to look out the window. She could just be friends with them. They both seemed nice enough. She hadn't really spent a lot of time with Tori, but their brief interactions were enough for her to make a snap decision. And anyone married to a ray of sunshine like Lea had to be pretty damn special. It would be nice to have friends. And people were attracted to their friends all the time, certainly.

It would take a lot of willpower to get over the initial disappointment and settle into a nice platonic groove, but she was confident in her abilities. She'd moved across the country on her own, she'd opened a restaurant during a pandemic, and she was thriving. Getting over a bad case of Feelings would be nothing compared to what she'd already accomplished.

She was finally starting to come out of the protective cocoon she'd built around herself after Eliza left. Most of their friends in Seattle had been couple friends, and leaving had saved them the trouble of choosing who got custody in the breakup. Being alone had been necessary to healing and discovering herself. She was a restaurant owner, she lived in Chicago, she had a nice apartment with nice neighbors who kept to themselves. She'd settled into a comfortable groove, and now it was time to test the strength by adding a new element.

Friends.

Married friends. A firefighter. A photographer.

She was confident.

When she got to work, she asked Evan for a wine recommendation. He asked what she was having, and she showed him the texts. He thought for a second and then came back with a bottle of white wine. He handed it to her and went back to prepping for the Sunday brunch crowd.

Janice examined the label. "What is it?"

"Pinot grigio," he said, then looked at her over the rims of his glasses. "If I tell you more, will you remember any of it?"

"I'll be honest, Evan, I can't guarantee I'll remember that much."

He shrugged. "It's not important. You're having pork, white wine will pair nicely. So. Who is the lucky lady?"

"Me." Janice put the bottle in her office. "I'm having dinner with Tori and Lea tonight."

Evan stopped prepping. "The Fire Lady?"

"Stop," she said. "It's not like that, it's just a friendly dinner. She's taken, and I'm not a homewrecker. I spent the day with her wife yesterday and I actually genuinely like her. She's doing a lot of work on the art for this place."

"Just friends." Evan's skepticism weighted down both words.

"Yes. And it's about time. You're the only friend I've made since coming to town, and you'd abandon me in a heartbeat if someplace trendier opened up."

Evan shook his head. "The restaurant does not make the chef trendy, the chef makes the restaurant trendy. I've put in too much work on this place to start over somewhere new."

She narrowed her eyes at him. "You're not the chef. You're the kitchen manager."

"Well, then. Find whoever is supposed to be the chef and let him know I'm doing his job."

Janice rolled her eyes and helped him prep. Sundays were always insanely busy, so she didn't have time to sit and drive herself crazy thinking about dinner. She told Evan that she planned to leave early so she could go home and get ready, and he waved her off.

"I'm the kitchen manager, I'm the cook, I'm running the whole show, I don't know what you pay all these other people for."

"I pay them to put up with you," she said, "and they charge a premium."

He bared his teeth at her and she gave him a quick hug as she left.

In the shower, she realized she hadn't asked Lea how fancy it was supposed to be. It was just going to be dinner in their apartment, so it would be casual. Right? But it was their first get-together as friends. She couldn't just throw on a sweater and jeans. She considered texting, but she didn't want to bug them this close to her arrival.

She went through her closet and took out her nicest blouse. It was silk, it was insanely expensive, and the buttons were fake pearl. She held it up in front of herself and imagined ringing their doorbell. It would certainly make an impression... and then she would spend the entire evening worried about dripping on it. And what if they went casual? She would feel completely ridiculous in something so flamboyant. It would ruin the evening.

Janice growled at the blouse and put it back in the closet, hiding it behind a coat. "Anxiety shirt. That's just going to be my anxiety shirt from now on."

She decided she would just choose an outfit she would feel comfortable in. Her favorite blue dress shirt and a pair of black slacks. It wasn't an outfit she would wear at work, but also something she would wear to the grocery store. The perfect balance, and hopefully complementary to whatever the Branigans were wearing.

At ten to eight, she called for a Lyft. It was easier to time her arrival that way, and she also felt a little grungy every time she took the train. Plus she was anxious about taking a bottle of wine on the train. She didn't think anyone would make a fuss, but there was no reason to add more hassle to her night.

They lived in Wrigleyville, just a few blocks away from the famous baseball field that give the neighborhood its name. She spent the ride telling herself to be calm, nervously twisting her hands around the neck of the wine bottle like she was choking it to death. It should be fine, it should be easy. The other night, she'd been nervous because she thought it was a date. Meeting Lea had been uncomfortable because she felt guilty.

This was just a dinner, and she had nothing to be nervous about.

The Lyft dropped her off two minutes before she was due. They lived in a courtyard apartment building, three wings forming a U around a fenced-in walkway. She determined which wing they lived in and stopped to check her reflection in the glass of the entrance. She ran her fingers through her hair. She'd worn it down, and wondered if that was a mistake. It looked good. It had dried naturally in waves, it wasn't too long, it looked casual. If she tried to put it up now, she would feel like she was going to work all night. So she dropped her hand, curled the fingers against the palm, and knocked against her hip.

"Stop stressing," she hissed as she yanked the door open and went inside. "It's going to be *fine*. There's no way for it to go badly, because the only thing required is to show up and eat. I can do that. It will be fine."

She climbed the two flights to their apartment, confident for the first and doubtful for the second. She knocked on their door and stepped back to reconsider her hair.

Tori answered before Janice could make any panicked decisions. Janice smiled, then raised her eyebrows and raked her eyes down Tori's body.

"Wow. You look amazing."

"Yeah, I clean up pretty well." Tori stepped aside to let her in. "Plus Lea picked my outfit."

"It's always nice to have a helping hand," Janice said.

"Not that you needed any help, apparently," Tori said.

The apartment was cozy, with a large living room that had been segmented into different spaces. The dinner table was in a nook with a bay window that overlooked the courtyard. The kitchen was directly across from the entrance, and Lea came around the counter already smiling. Her dress was bright red with small white shapes all over it, cut low in the chest and high on the leg. If she hadn't been wearing a tee-shirt underneath it would have been borderline obscene. Not that Janice would have complained. She held her arms out in greeting as she crossed the room.

"You made it!" Lea said, wrapping Janice in a hug without asking. She also wasn't going to complain about that. "You look wonderful!"

"Same all around," Janice said.

Lea stepped back and looked down at herself. "Do you like?" She plucked the dress between her fingers and held it out, doing a spin. "Tori calls it my strawberry dress. Because of the little specks."

"I can see it." She had a sudden realization. "Shit! I was going to get the measurements for the restaurant so you can~"

"No!" Lea said, holding up both hands to stop her. "No. You forgot for a reason. It is because tonight is about friends and fun and food. Not work. I would not allow you to talk about it even if you had brought the measurements."

Janice sighed, irritated but deciding to let it go. "Uh, well. I did remember to bring something more important." She held up the wine. "I've been told this will go well with the amazing meal I've been smelling since Tori opened the door."

Tori took the bottle. "Ah, an excellent choice. It's... wine.

White wine, if I'm not mistaken."

"I didn't know we had a connoisseur in the house," Lea said with a smirk. "Go get the glasses and prepare the plates. Janice, you're with me."

She slipped an arm around Janice's and walked her to the dining room. The table was draped in a forest green cloth with a floral arrangement in the center and two tall candles. Janice was grateful for the escort because there were three place settings and she wasn't entirely sure which one she was supposed to take. Lea guided her to the chair with her back to the window.

"Will this be suitable, madam?" Lea said, putting on a softer voice.

"I think it would do just fine."

Lea winked and stepped back. "Your waitress will be with you shortly."

Janice took her seat. She twisted to look out the window, which looked out over the courtyard. The view wouldn't win any awards, but it was superb for people-watching in other side of the building. It always surprised her how people in buildings like this rarely seemed to bother with curtains. She could see people watching television, a woman on a Zoom call despite the hour, a man watching *The Office* on a Peloton, an elderly couple in recliners facing the flicker of a television...

She turned back around and looked into the kitchen. Lea was standing close to Tori, whispering something to her. Tori nodded, pecked Lea's hairline, and picked up two plates. Lea picked up the glasses and they returned to the dining room together.

Tori delivered the plate to Janice. "*Lechon asado*, which is Cuban roast pork, courtesy of Lea Contreras-Branigan."

"It smells wonderful," Janice said.

Lea beamed proudly and sat to Janice's left, while Tori returned to the kitchen to get her plate and drink. She brought it back and sat across from Janice. Janice picked up her glass and held it out.

"Why don't we start with a toast? To new friends."

"Ah!" Lea looked at Tori, and a message seemed to pass between them. Tori may have shrugged, or it may have just been the way the candlelight flickered at that moment. Whatever they shared, Lea picked up her own glass. "Of course! A wonderful sentiment. To new friends!"

Tori tapped her glass against theirs.

"Is everything okay?" Janice asked. "Did I say something wrong?"

"No, no, no," Lea said a little too quickly. "It's just that, um..."

She leaned forward and her hair fell across her face, preventing Janice from seeing any expression she might have made. Tori raised her eyebrows in response to whatever had been silently asked. She took a sip of her wine, shrugged, and made a gesture that Janice interpreted as 'go ahead.'

"You guys are freaking me out a little," Janice admitted.

"Sorry," Lea said. "It's just that we've had, um, a few conversations behind your back." She wrinkled her nose and narrowed her eyes in apology. It was cute enough that it worked. "We have a confession to make. We know that when you originally asked Tori to dinner, it was meant to be a date."

Janice felt a sudden chill, which was followed by a burning in her cheeks. "Oh. Shit."

"No, don't... please don't be upset!" Lea held up a hand to stop Janice from saying anything. "I-it's fine. We're all friends here, right? We just toasted! That's binding. All right? So. We didn't know until after the fact. I realized when I saw your reaction to me being there. Tori didn't figure it out until I explained it to her."

"I'm still... I'm so sorry. If I had known she was married~"

Lea shook her head, chuckling. "Don't worry. Please. You're freaking out. Shit. I should have thought more about how I was going to do this." She sat back in her chair. "I was supposed to do it yesterday during our excursion, but Tori called it off at the last second. She thought it would be better to ask tonight. I should have been preparing!"

Janice frowned. "Preparing what? What were you supposed to do yesterday?"

Lea looked at Tori. Tori said, "I can take over if you want."

"No, it's fine." Janice took a drink of wine, wet her lips, and focused on Janice. "Once Tori was informed about your intentions, I asked her if she was interested. In a world where I didn't exist, or we weren't married, would she have accepted your invitation to dinner. She said she would. She finds you very attractive and was flattered you asked her out."

"If you think this is easing the sting of rejection, it's really not." Janice chuckled. "I appreciate the effort, but really. You don't have to~"

Lea stopped her with a raised hand again. "And," she said, "I admitted that I also found you attractive. And having spent the day with you, I think you're a wonderful person that I would be glad to have as a friend."

Tori said, "Or..."

Janice looked at Tori. Then she looked back at Lea, who was staring at her with an odd intensity. It was like they'd asked a question and expected her to answer.

"Or?" Janice repeated.

Lea lifted her shoulders in a shrug. "We're mature adults. Tori and I are very secure in our relationship. We know how we feel about each other." She smiled at Tori and reached out for her. Tori took her hand. Lea looked back at Janice. "And we know how we feel about you. And how *you* feel for *Tori*. So if you also find *me* attractive..."

"I do," Janice said quietly, cautiously.

She'd figured out what they were implying, but she didn't want to be the one to say it. Her heart was in her throat. It was a struggle to keep her breathing steady. She didn't want them to think she was panicked, but she was right on the edge. She rested her hands on the table and hoped the hard surface would keep them from trembling.

Lea cleared her throat. She looked at Tori again. Tori wet her lips.

"Would you like to have sex with us, Janice?"

Janice finished her wine and hoped whatever expression she wore didn't read as nauseous. She appreciated the bluntness, and decided to answer in kind.

"Very much. Yes."

Tori looked relieved. Lea looked overjoyed.

CHAPTER SEVEN

SILENCE SETTLED over the table. Lea had sagged back against her chair, both hands folded in front of her smiling lips, looking at her wife. Tori was smiling like someone who had been dreading something all week and was finally finished with it. Janice still had her hands on the table, looking between both of them, waiting for some prompt or indication of what would happen next.

"So..." Janice finally said. "Did you mean... n-now?"

Lea sat up. "Oh! No, no, no. I mean. I don't..." She looked at Tori for confirmation, then shook her head. "No. We didn't... I mean, you didn't come over expecting..."

"Right," Janice said, thinking about the underwear she'd chosen for the evening. "I thought it would just be dinner with friends."

"Right." Lea nodded emphatically. "And, and, and we're just springing this on you out of the blue. You need time to really think it over."

Janice said, "Oh. No I don't. I mean... I was attracted to Tori instantly. And you. You're gorgeous. And getting to know you has only made you more attractive. If I had the chance to be with either of you, I'd jump at it. And being with both of you is... it's..." She exhaled sharply and reached for her empty glass. "Oh."

Tori said, "Oh, let me..."

She went into the kitchen and returned with the bottle. She refilled Janice's glass, then topped off hers and Lea's before she sat back down.

"Thank you." Janice took a drink, let it sit on her tongue, then swallowed. "I'm not going to say no. I'm just saying when."

"Whenever you want." Lea was flushed now, her voice breathless.

Tori cleared her throat. "How about this? We eat this dinner Lea prepared for us, because it smells absolutely wonderful. Then we go over to the couch and we discuss how we'll go about this. I think being blunt and upfront about everything will make the whole experience better for all of us."

"Agreed."

"I third," Lea said. "I hope you like it, Janice."

Janice smiled. "No offense, because I know you worked hard on it, but there's no way I'm going to be thinking about the food right now."

Tori and Lea both laughed.

With the tension eased, they started eating. Janice looked up from her plate, first at Tori and then at Lea, and cleared her throat.

"I'm not sure there's a good transition subject from... that. So I suppose I'll just ask how you two met."

Lea grinned. "At a photo shoot. I was hired to photograph frontline workers for a magazine. Tori showed up, and the moment I saw her in her uniform..."

Janice shook her head. "That thing is a threat to public safety."

"It's literally my work clothes," Tori said.

Janice laughed. "Okay. We'll stop objectifying you."

"If that's what you really want," Lea teased.

Tori considered it, shrugged. "Fine. But it's not fair that neither of you have uniforms so I can't return the favor."

Janice laughed and realized the tension she'd been carrying all day had faded. Part of it was having all the cards on the table and knowing exactly where she stood with these women. The wine helped, too. She would have to thank Evan for providing it. As the meal went on, Tori became more relaxed and started smiling more, laughing easier. Lea's accent became more pronounced, and she started injecting more Spanish words into conversation which required Tori to translate.

Near the end of the meal, Lea got up and went to an entertainment center on the bookshelf. At some point during the night she had lost her shoes. Janice noticed that she walked on the balls of her feet with her heels in the air, like she was trying to tiptoe. She plugged her phone into the center piece, scrolled across the screen, and then began dancing before the music started. It was a pop song with a touch of disco, something Janice had never heard but she couldn't help moving her head to the beat.

Lea, on the other hand, went into a full-on dance routine between the living room and kitchen. She swept her hand through her hair, kicked up the ends of her dress, swayed left to right, swung her hips, and basically seemed to have been transported to her own private club.

Janice smiled, but looked at Tori to see if she was worried. "Has she had a little too much?"

Tori laughed and shook her head. "She just gets like this. Especially with Dua Lipa."

"Come and dance with me, Victoria," Lea said.

Tori said, "We're in the middle of dinner."

Janice said, "It's fine, you can dance with her."

"Are you sure? It feels rude."

"Are you kidding?" She gestured at Lea, still swaying by herself next to the couch. "That woman dancing alone is practically a crime. Go on."

Lea held out her arms and waved her fingers at Tori. "You heard the woman. We don't want to be criminals, do we?"

Tori took another drink of wine, then went to her wife. Lea chuckled victoriously and wrapped her arms around Tori's waist. The song ended and then began again, apparently on a loop. On the second listen, Janice realized that the chorus was in French and Lea was singing along. Heat rose in Janice's cheeks and she finished off her wine. A sexy Cuban woman who wanted her singing in French and dancing like that was a trigger she hadn't realized she had.

The song was apparently fairly short, as it started again as Janice got out of her seat. She watched Tori and Janice dance with each other as she crossed the room. There wasn't a lot of distance to cover, but it seemed like it took her ten minutes to reach them. Lea smiled over Tori's shoulder and motioned her closer, then reached out to her.

"Can I cut in?" Janice asked, because that seemed like an appropriate thing to say at this highly inappropriate moment.

"Which one of us are you asking?" Tori asked.

"I'm not sure I care."

Tori leaned in and kissed Lea, then stepped out of the way. Janice moved into the space she had vacated, and suddenly Lea was pressed against her. Standing so close, and in this light, her eyes were remarkably green, unbelievably green. The wine had made her eyelids heavy but she was still locked in on Janice's face with unwavering steadiness. She was also still mouthing the lyrics of the song.

Lea's hands were on Janice's hips. Suddenly another pair of hands were on her shoulders. She turned and looked up. Tori was tall. She was so tall, and now she towered over both of them. Janice returned her stare, then turned and looked at Lea. She and Lea were the same height. Lea's eyebrow twitched and she lifted her head slightly.

Janice took it as an invitation.

She pressed her lips to Lea's during a lull in the song, and her heartbeat swelled to fill the silence. Lea curled her fingers so that Janice could feel the scrape of nails through her shirt, and then she moved her hands to the small of Janice's back and pulled her closer. Lea moaned and opened her mouth, and her tongue swept into Janice's mouth, suddenly taking the position of aggressor. Janice gasped in surprise and returned the kiss.

She was very aware of Tori's presence at her back, her large hands on her shoulders and then on her neck, then in her hair. The hand tightened and pulled gently, breaking the kiss so abruptly that Janice gasped. She turned, lips still parted, and turned her head. Tori leaned forward and captured her mouth, still holding her hair as Lea started kissing her cheek and her neck.

Lea was still dancing, still moving her body, but now her breasts and hips moved against Janice's. Her hands were roaming now. She explored Janice's hips, moved up across her ribcage, cupped her breasts through her blouse.

Janice ended the kiss with Tori and cupped the back of Lea's head with one hand, reaching back to put her other hand on Tori's hip.

"Are you okay?" Tori's voice was barely audible over the music.

Janice nodded. "Very okay." She pulled gently on Lea's hair, raising her head up so she would also be part of the conversation. "I want this to happen tonight."

Lea stood up straighter. She suddenly looked much more sober. "Are you sure?" She pushed her hair out of her face. She cut a glance at Tori, then looked back at Janice. "We don't want you to do anything you're not comfortable with."

"If we don't do this tonight," Janice said, "I'm not going to be able to focus on anything else until it happens." She cupped Lea's face and leaned in, kissed her softly. Tori's hands slid across her back, over her shoulders and down her spine. She broke the kiss and stroked her fingers over the impossibly soft skin of Lea's cheek. "I want it to happen tonight," she said again.

"Me too," Tori said.

Lea exhaled sharply, her smile making it sound almost like a laugh. "Okay."

"Just don't judge me on my underwear."

Tori laughed and kissed Janice's cheek. Janice turned her head and kissed her properly, and Lea pressed up tight against her, one hand sliding down to her ass. Janice kept one hand on each of them, eyes closed, listening to the way her heartbeat had synced to the rhythm of the song.

She wondered how many times it would repeat before the night ended, and if her heart could keep up with it.

There was only one way to find out.

They left the living room light on and the bedroom light off as they transitioned across the apartment. The normal, everyday glow of the overheads became faded and golden by the time it reached the bed. The room was still lit well enough that Janice could see a book and a cup of water on one nightstand, hand cream and the coiled end of a phone charger on the other. This was undeniably the bed of a married couple, a fact that caused alarm bells to sound in some deep recess of her mind. *THIS IS WRONG!*, the voice shouted. *You are about to have an affair! Two affairs! At the same time!*

Tori stopped behind her and put her hands on Janice's shoulders. "Are you still okay with this?"

"Yes," Janice said, and the word silenced the alarms.

She turned around and stretched up to press her lips to Tori's. Lea moved around them to press against Janice from behind. She reached around to grab Tori's waist, pulled her forward, and pinned Janice between them. Janice moaned when Lea began kissing her neck. Her head swam. For a moment, she was afraid she would lose her balance, but she was completely surrounded and knew she was safe even if her legs gave out.

"What do you want?" Lea asked, her whisper sounding

impossibly loud next to her ear.

Janice pulled away from Tori and turned to face Lea. "I want to watch you undress each other."

Lea bit her lip and looked at Tori. There was something different about her eyes now. They seemed darker, more intense. More animalistic. Lea reached out and caressed Tori's cheek, brushed her fingers across her lips, and then whispered something in Spanish. Janice retreated a step, and Tori moved to take her place, wrapping Lea in an embrace and kissing her hard. Tori bent her knees and lifted, and Lea wrapped her legs around Tori's waist, allowing herself to be carried to the bed without breaking the kiss. Janice moved to stand at the foot of the bed.

Tori bent down to place Lea on the mattress, then sat up and ran her hands over her wife's body. Lea grinned and lifted her arms as Tori's fingers slowly moved over the row of buttons running down the front of her dress. She plucked each one free and peeled the cloth away, revealing tan skin and two strips of black lace underwear. When the last button was undone, Lea sat up to shrug it off her shoulders.

Janice licked her lips, tasting Lea's lipstick, and moved one hand between her legs. She pressed her hand against the crotch of her slacks as she watched Tori lay on top of Lea and kiss her chest, her belly, and then down to her thighs. Lea watched, transfixed, then turned her head to look at Janice. She smiled. Janice smiled back, hoping she didn't look nervous or uncertain.

"Nice underwear," Janice said. Her voice shook, and she cleared her throat in an attempt to steady it. "Looks like you were hoping for this to happen tonight."

"I wanted you very much," Lea admitted. Her voice was like honey and cinnamon, smooth with a bite, and Janice wanted to spend all night repeating it in her head to lock in that sound.

Tori was between Lea's legs now. She knelt on the floor next to the bed and pulled Lea to her, resting Lea's legs on her shoulders, and kissed her thighs. Lea propped herself up on her elbows.

"It's okay if you want to just watch us," she said to Janice.

"No..." Janice walked to the other side of the bed. She stopped long enough to unbutton her pants and push them down, then climbed onto the bed. She knelt on the mattress behind Lea and acted as a cushion for her. Lea rested her shoulders against Janice's chest and purred contentedly. Janice watched Tori as her hands moved blindly, finding the clasp of Lea's bra and releasing it. She hooked her finger under one strap and Lea lifted her arms so it could be pulled off of her. Her breasts were small but perfect, with large dark nipples. Janice took one breast in her hand, squeezed, and kissed Lea's hair. She looked down and locked eyes with Tori...

...who brushed her cheek over Lea's thigh and looked up to see two beautiful women staring down at her. Janice's cheeks were flushed, her eyes wide and her lips parted. Her hand cupped Lea's breast and squeezed, then she teased the hard nipple with her fingers. Lea rolled her eyes back and squirmed in response, baring her teeth and making the soft sounds of impatience that Tori knew so well. She wet her lips and pressed a kiss to the lace of Lea's underwear, then used her thumb to push it aside. Lea sucked in air through her teeth when Tori's finger brushed her.

Tori felt a thrill doing this while Janice watched. Sex with Lea was always amazing, but to be watched like this seemed to be awakening an exhibitionist or voyeuristic side of herself that she'd never known existed. With that in mind, she looked past Lea and focused on Janice as she used the flat of her tongue to tease Lea's lips. Lea...

...squirmed underneath her and muttered, "Ay, *qué rico*..." She reached up with one hand, blindly groping for Janice, while her other hand went to the back of Tori's head. "Deeper," she whispered, and then Janice was kissing her, and she could only moan. Janice's hand left her breast, and she whimpered in protest until she felt it on her belly, and then she felt Tori lift up. She looked down in time to see Janice put two fingers into Tori's mouth.

"Fuck," she moaned, bracing herself for what was going to happen next.

Tori's tongue was back on her, inside her, and then Janice's wet fingers brushed through her pubic hair and found her clit. Janice stroked with her middle finger as she kissed Lea's neck. Her other hand came up around Lea's other side to embrace her, and Lea guided that hand to her breast. Janice took the hint and resumed teasing her nipple while her other hand conspired with Tori's tongue.

She came much faster than she expected, hoped, or wanted, and she held onto both women desperately, as if clinging to them would stop the orgasm. She whispered, "Wait, wait, wait," to herself, but it was a lost cause. She heard Tori - "It's okay, baby..." - and twisted to press her face against the smooth material of Janice's shirt to muffle her cry. Her legs tightened, but Tori...

...lifted up in time to prevent herself from being trapped. She kissed the back of Janice's hand, traveling up her arm until she was lying on top of Lea and kissing Janice. She hadn't kissed anyone but Lea in six years - technically closer to seven years - and there had been a physical reaction to strange lips the first time she kissed Janice. But now her body seemed to have acclimated, and now she could taste both Janice and Lea's lipstick on Janice's mouth, and the combination made her head swim.

While she kissed Janice's lips, Lea had twisted to kiss Janice's breasts through her shirt. Lea lifted up and looked at Tori.

"Am I the only one not wearing clothes?"

"I took my pants off," Janice said.

"*Por Dios*, Victoria!" Lea began pulling at Tori's clothes. "She said she wanted to watch us to undress each other."

Tori said, "I got distracted."

"I can't hold that against her." Janice...

...slipped away from Lea and repositioned herself against the headboard, their pillows under her. Lea squirmed up so she was in the middle of the bed and folded her legs under her. Tori joined her, and they kissed as Lea pushed the shirt off Tori's shoulders. Her broad shoulders, which tapered down to muscular, tanned arms with biceps that flexed as she took Lea in her arms to kiss her again.

Janice moved her legs apart and put her hand between her legs, rubbing herself as she watched Tori's clothes slowly come off. She looked like a normal, slender woman in her clothes, but nudity revealed a topographical map of tight muscles that moved and clenched. They kissed each other as Lea undid her wife's clothes with easy familiarity. Janice wet her fingers again, tasting Lea on them, and slipped them into her underwear.

Tori's bra came off, and Lea bowed to take a nipple into her mouth. Tori arched her back and ran her fingers through Lea's hair, then lifted her eyes to see what Janice was doing.

"Hi," Tori said.

"Hey," Janice said, smiling, shuddering. "You're both so beautiful."

Lea lifted her head. "We undressed each other," she said, moving her hands to cup Tori's ass. "Now what should we do?"

Janice inhaled, let out the breath, and pulled her hand out of her underwear.

"Fuck me."

The Branigans smiled and crawled to her.

Chapter Eight

LEA WAS confused before she even opened her eyes. She could smell breakfast cooking, the delicious scent was likely what drew her from such a deep sleep, but Tori was still spooning her in bed. Or no... She knew what it felt like to be held by Tori. These arms were wrong, the body pressed against her was wrong. She slid her hand up the forearm across her waist and had flashes of the night before: a tongue in her mouth and lips on her neck, so many fingers all over her, watching someone else's hands grab Tori's hair in a kiss.

She smiled and squirmed around so that she was lying on her back. Her movement woke Janice, whose eyelids fluttered and then opened, then focused. Her face remained neutral, but Lea felt as if she could see a whole script of unsaid words running behind her eyes.

"Morning," Janice said quietly.

"Hi." Lea leaned in and kissed Janice's cheek, then her lips. "Are you okay?"

Janice scanned the room. "Yeah. I think so." She ran her hand up Lea's back. "Are you? Is Tori? Are... i-is everything~"

"You can ask her yourself over breakfast," Lea said. "But I assume the fact that she's making breakfast is a good sign."

"Yeah?"

"Mm-hmm." Lea hunched her shoulders and pushed her feet

out, stretching until her joints quietly popped. "Shower. Spare toothbrush is in the top right drawer. Towels are on a shelf, you'll see them. And, um..." She lifted her head and pointed to a dresser. "Tori has clothes in there. You can borrow something so you don't have to wear last night's clothes."

"Okay."

The uncertainty had returned to her voice. "Hey," Lea said softly, stroking her cheek until Janice looked at her again. "You were so confident last night. Are you sure you're okay?"

"Yeah. Last night was... last night. There was a lot of energy flying around last night. It was easy to get swept up. I wanted everything that happened to happen. A part of me is just worried that I pulled you or Tori along in my wake."

Lea sat up enough to hug her. "You didn't do anything wrong. We both... we *all* wanted last night to happen. The only question was when it would happen, and we definitely don't blame you for not wanting to wait. If anyone is guilty of coercion, it's me. I knew what I was doing when I put on that song."

Janice laughed. "Good. Because that was basically entrapment." She touched Lea's cheek. "Can I kiss you?"

"Mm-hmm."

They kissed, and then Janice pulled back with a smile. "Shower. Towels on a shelf. Toothbrush in the top right drawer."

"Yes."

"Okay... be right back."

Lea watched her get out of bed, taking time to admire the curve of her hips and everything that branched out from them. She'd spent a good amount of time appreciating each part up close the night before, but it was a whole new experience to see her move across the room. Her blonde hair was a tangled mess, and her legs were apparently still half-asleep because she stumbled and crossed her right foot in front of her left which made her wobble a bit. Lea found that just as erotic as her dance.

Once the shower started, Lea spread her feet apart under the blanket and stretched again. They had both treated her so well last night... she remembered one all too brief interlude where they had both been inside her at the same time, a memory that made her shudder. But the memory she was going to treasure would be watching them with each other. Seeing Tori make love to a beautiful woman. Seeing another woman experience Tori's skills for the first time.

She had stretched out on her side of the bed and masturbated as she watched Tori go down on Janice, her eyes running along the length of Janice's body to watch her face change. She had tried to guess what Tori was doing to her, then realized she didn't have to guess. She had scooted closer and kissed Janice's cheek, then whispered in her ear, "Tell me what she's doing."

Janice hadn't done very well as a commentator, but even hearing her try - "She's... l-licking me..." followed by incoherent groaning and a hand groping for Lea's - was enough to cause shivers even now, the next morning.

Lea pulled Tori's pillow to her, curling on her side and pressing her face against the pillowcase, breathing deeply, falling back to sleep with a smile on her face.

Tori glanced up when she saw the bedroom door crack open and smiled at the hesitation before it opened all the way. Janice came out with her hair still wet, wearing a navy blue fire department T-shirt and a pair of her sweatpants. It was an outfit she'd seen Lea wear on countless mornings, and seeing this relative stranger in it was surreal. Janice quietly closed the door behind her and continued down the hall, through the living room, on bare feet.

"Good morning," she whispered.

"You don't have to whisper," Tori said at normal volume. "Lea's asleep?"

Janice nodded.

Tori chuckled. "Yeah. She won't wake up. All that energy you saw last night? She borrowed that from today. She can go for hours but the next day she's dead to the world until lunch."

"Oh. Okay."

Tori held up a coffee pot, and Janice nodded. Tori filled a mug and handed it to her.

"Thank you." She looked at the stove, the breakfast items still scattered on the counter. "I don't know the etiquette. Do I get breakfast?"

"Absolutely. We're good hosts. I was waiting to find out how you prefer your eggs."

"What's your specialty?"

Tori grinned. "Poached."

"Show-off," Janice said.

Tori laughed and shrugged. "It's a little-known fact about firefighters. We all get very good at cooking. Bacon or sausage?"

"Let's just make the whole breakfast dealer's choice."

"I can do that." She started prepping the eggs. "So. Are you okay? With everything that happened last night? We can do a post-game if you need to."

Janice looked out the window, chewing on her bottom lip. Tori let her think, focused on the food. Finally Janice looked back at her.

"I don't think so. I'm really glad it happened. As long as the two of you are both happy with what happened..."

"We're more than happy," Tori said. "You fell asleep first." She paused and remembered Janice, sweaty and still breathing hard, passing out between them. Her head was on Lea's breast, and Tori was still twitching from her last orgasm. "We kissed right over your head. The last thing Lea said to me before she fell asleep was 'thank you' and 'I love you so much'. So while I try not to put words in her mouth, I think it's safe to say she's happy with what happened."

Janice's face was flush, and she was smiling in a way that was almost delirious. "Good. Good, I'm... I'm really glad. I talked to her when I first woke up, and she was definitely okay with it. I'm just overthinking. And just being extra certain, you know? Just to cover the bases. It's nice when something you want so much is, um... reciprocated."

"Definitely. The other way sucks."

Janice looked down into her coffee. "So is it... going to happen again?"

Tori hesitated with a spoon over the pot. "Well. I have a shift starting at noon. Lea probably wouldn't mind being woken up for that~"

"No, no." Janice laughed. "I mean. I'm not opposed. I meant in general. Is this going to be a thing that happens? Or was it a thing that happened, and going forward we're just friends who happened to fuck that one time?"

"Oh." Tori furrowed her brow. She and Lea had talked about it so often, they never spent much time thinking about afterward. She'd been so nervous about breaching the subject that she hadn't seriously considered the next step. "That's something that I definitely have to talk over with Lea before I said anything."

"Right, of course," Janice said. "I understand. When you do talk about it, just for the record, I'm fine with whatever the two of you decide. I never... I didn't think this was..." She gestured vaguely. "I was happy with the idea of just being your friend. If that's what happens from now on, I'll still be getting what I wanted. Best of both worlds."

Tori chuckled. "Your vote is registered." She moved the poached eggs to a plate and delivered it to Janice. "And for the record, I wouldn't be upset if Lea wanted to do it again."

Their eyes met and they held each other's gaze for a long moment. Janice smiled, awkward, and Tori stepped back as she let go of the plate.

"Um. Condiments? Drink? We have orange juice, milk..."

"I'll take an orange juice."

Tori poured her a glass. "And, um, if you don't mind me abandoning you, I would like to hop in the shower before~"

Janice waved her off. "Go, go. I hope I left you some hot water."

"If not, I'll blame the building, not you. I'll be right back."

She considered kissing Janice before she left, but she couldn't decide if lips or cheek would be appropriate. If a kiss was appropriate at all. Which it probably wasn't. So she simply fled into the bedroom.

Lea was mostly wrapped in the blankets, but her chest was exposed along with the length of one bent leg. Tori went to the bed and grabbed the foot. She pinched the little toe, then used it to lift the foot and shake it. Lea growl-groaned into the pillow, then yanked her foot away. She kept her cheek pressed against the pillow but opened one eye.

"What do you want?" she said.

"I want to shower with you."

Lea made a 'harrumph' sound, pushed the pillow away, and forced herself upright as if she was a puppet with tangled strings.

"As long as you have a good reason," she grumbled.

She scooted off the mattress and followed Tori into the bathroom. Tori was stepping out of her pants by the time Lea joined her, leaning past her to turn on the water. They stepped into the tub together, positioning themselves so the spray hit both of them instead of being blocked by Tori's shoulders. Lea put her arms around Tori's waist and sagged against her. Tori cupped her hands to gather the water and then carefully spilled it over Lea's hair.

"Are we okay?" she asked.

"I'm very okay." Lea tilted her head back. "You?"

Tori grinned. "Yeah. Very okay." She kissed Lea softly and ran her fingers through her hair.

"What about Janice?"

"I think she's very okay, too." Tori left Lea's hair behind and had moved on to idly washing her arms. "She asked if we could do it again."

Lea nodded, shrugging. "Sure. You don't have to go in until noon, right?"

Tori laughed. "You and I are definitely made for each other. She didn't mean now, she meant... in the future. She's happy to just be our friend, but she wanted to know if this was a one-time thing or if it's going to be a, um, a thing we do sometimes."

"Oh." Lea thought about it. "I'd like it to be a thing we do."

Tori leaned down and brushed her lips across Lea's. "Yeah? You want to fuck her again?"

"I want to see her fuck you again," Lea whispered back, then kissed Tori.

They kissed for a bit, Tori keeping her mind on where her feet were planted so she didn't slip. When the kiss ended, she smoothed Lea's hair back.

"Okay. Then this was just the first time it happened."

"Mm-hmm. I like that."

Tori nodded. "Me too."

They finished showering, helping each other with the hard to reach places. Tori helped Lea towel off, then Lea returned the favor. By the time they returned to the kitchen, Janice had finished washing the plates and silverware from breakfast.

"You didn't have to do that," Tori said.

"If you don't cook, you clean," Janice said. "Standard house rules. I left the cookware stuff because Lea hadn't eaten yet."

Lea said, "So considerate. I usually just have yogurt and some fruit. But thank you. And good morning." She walked up to Janice and gave her a lingering good morning kiss.

Janice tensed, eyes wide and sweeping over to look at Tori.

Tori grinned. "I didn't get jealous over the places she kissed you last night, I'm not going to make a fuss about the lips."

"It's just a proper good morning," Lea said. "It's why toothpaste is so minty."

"Oh is *that* why," Tori said.

"Mm-hmm."

Janice settled back on her stool. "Can I ask you something, Lea?" She nodded as she took a yogurt out of the fridge. "Who is Rico?"

Lea frowned. She looked at Tori, who was equally confused.

"I don't know any Rico," Lea said.

"You said the name a couple of times last night."

Lea tilted her head to the side. "I did?"

Tori realized what Janice was talking about and laughed. Lea jumped, startled. Tori looked at Lea and said, "Ay, *qué rico.*"

Lea understood. "Oh my god! Ay, *qué rico!*" She laughed and put the back of her hand against her mouth.

Janice smiled uncomfortably. "Right... So...?"

"It's, um..." Lea waved her spoon in the air like a baton. "Something I say. In the moment. It means 'oh, how lovely' or delightful..."

"Or tasty," Tori said.

"Or tasty," Lea confirmed with a bright smile, touching her tongue to her top lip. "Although that would be *qué rica*, since I am referring to someone feminine. But yes, Janice, technically I suppose to answer your question... *you* were Rico."

Tori grinned. "Sounds like someone just got a nickname."

Janice covered her face and laughed. "Oh, God. I'm sorry I asked."

"Oh it's not so bad. Who doesn't want to be lovely, delightful, and tasty?" She winked and licked the cup of her spoon.

CHAPTER NINE

JANICE WASN'T sure how to extricate herself from the apartment with grace, so she was relieved when Lea went back to bed and gave her an out. Tori let her borrow the department shirt to wear home - "Might as well keep it, actually. I have at least two dozen of them. And it looks good on you."

Janice took the L home, staring out the window at the city passing by and reliving some of the greatest hits of the night before. The clothes she'd worn to the apartment were folded neatly on her lap. She ran her fingers over the buttons of the blouse and remembered Lea's fingers undoing them just a few hours earlier. She remembered Tori's hand against the seat of her pants, squeezing. The underwear in her pocket had been brushed by Lea's cheek and Tori's lips before they finally came off.

The thoughts kept her distracted for the twenty minute ride. She didn't snap out of it until she heard the familiar automated voice - "This is Harrison" - and she jumped out of her seat to get out the doors on time. She checked her watch as she climbed the stairs to the street. Canvas didn't open until lunchtime on Mondays, so she had an hour to go home, maybe catch a catnap, and try to find some version of normal to get her through the day.

Two hours later, sitting in her office next to the kitchen, she was still distracted. She was in her own clothes. She was in a place that was more familiar to her than her own apartment. The further away she got from the Branigans and their apartment, the less real it seemed. She heard the exterior door open and closed and looked out into the kitchen to see Evan had arrived.

"Evan." He glanced up and she waved him in. "Come here."

He crossed the kitchen without taking off his coat. "Morning, boss. How'd dinner with the fire lady go?"

"Close the door," she said.

He raised his eyebrows and closed the door. "Is this a good door-closing or a~"

"We had sex."

Evan froze with his hand still on the knob. "I'm sorry? You had sex with the fire lady? Wasn't her wife there?"

"Yep." She pressed her lips together.

"So where~" His eyes widened. "Oh no. You *didn't*."

She smiled awkwardly, took a breath, and let it out in a single gust. "Yeah."

"How.. h-how did… w-was it, like, a spontaneous~"

"No. They ambushed me. But a good ambush. Um, it wasn't…" She pushed her hands into her hair, grabbed two handfuls, and shook. "I thought saying it out loud would make it make sense. But it's just tangling everything up even more."

Evan leaned against the wall. "Let's focus on the important questions. How awkward were things between you all this morning?"

"Not at all. It was great. Fire la~ Tori made me poached eggs. I think they fucked in the shower while I was doing the dishes." She heard what she'd just said. "Oh, God. I shouldn't be telling you all of this. It's private, it's their private…"

He held up his hands. "Everything in here is vaulted. You can trust that. Second important question… how was the sex?"

She sagged back against her seat. "Oh my God."

"Oh, okay," Evan said.

"Oh. My *Go-ho-od*." She put a hand to her chest and mimed gasping for air. "Either one of them would have been a top five. But together, I may have to reorganize everything."

Evan grinned. "Well, good for you. I was starting to worry you were destined to be one of those people who marry their business. I'm glad you got back out there."

"Uh huh," she said.

"You… don't sound glad."

Janice leaned forward. "It's weird. Right? Threesomes? Who does threesomes?"

"I've done threesomes," he said. "It's one of the perks of being bisexual. Same rules apply as in a two-some. As long as everyone goes in happy and ends up happy, there's no reason to make it weird."

"I guess..."

There was a knock on the door and Evan stepped aside so it could open. The hostess, Malinda, poked her head around the corner.

"Miss Kozak? There's a woman here? I told her we're not open yet, but she said she's looking for someone named Rico...?"

Janice's cheeks burst into flames, or so it felt. Evan and Malinda were both looking at her confused, but she thought she could see a twinge of understanding in Evan's eyes. He had an idea who might be outside, but he couldn't put the pieces together. Janice got out of her chair and smoothed a hand over her hair.

"Thanks, Malinda. Tell her I'll be right out."

Malinda left. Evan tilted his head to the side.

"Rico...?"

"No."

"Oh, come on, you've got to explain *Rico*. What the hell could that possibly mean? How do you get a nickname like *Rico* in the space of one~"

She held up a finger, then pointed at the open door, then drew her finger across her lips.

"Vault door is open," she said. "That means everything is locked down. Got it?"

"Crystal," he said. "But you can't stop me from speculating quietly inside my head."

She sighed and left him to his speculation.

As predicted, Lea was standing in the dining room, using a tablet to take photos of the walls. She smiled when Janice came out of the kitchen.

"Hey!"

"No Rico," Janice said under her breath. "Not here. Okay?"

Lea's smile fell. "I'm sorry. I hope I didn't cause any problems. I thought it would be cute." She put her hand on Janice's arm. "I'm sorry. It won't happen again."

"It's okay. I'm not angry. I just..." She looked at Malinda. The hostess stand was out of earshot, but the girl was clearly watching them. "It's fine. Um, what's up?"

"Well, I had a client cancel, and I was just two L stops short of here. So I decided to come out and get the measurements myself. Save you a trip."

"Thank you. That's very sweet."

Lea took a moment to adjust, hugging her tablet to her chest, clearly still distraught at potentially crossing a line. She cleared her throat and scanned the room.

"Ahem. Well. I also thought it would be good to really look at the space again. Last time I was here, I didn't look at it with a professional eye. And now that we know what we have, it's easier to envision the finished product. Like I'm thinking the suffragettes here..." She framed a section of the wall. "That way you can see it from almost every seat, and as soon as you enter."

"I love that," Janice said. "Yeah."

"And the moose blowing a bubble." She turned. "We can put that there. Sort of a hidden treasure for regular customers. Oh, and I've spoken with the college. We'll display every piece with the names of the artists to be sure they get proper credit for their work."

Janice nodded. "That all sounds wonderful. And yes, absolutely, the suffragettes should be the focus. I love that idea. Then we can put smaller pieces here, so each table can have their own unique piece."

"Mm-hmm." Lea turned in a slow circle. "The statues may work best by the window to the kitchen here. And then..." She pointed at the cash register. "A big landscape behind the counter there. Something that really screams *Chicago*, you know? Maybe the L or something. We want people to know this is a local restaurant. You might not have roots here, but you're building. You're growing branches."

Janice smiled. "I love that."

"Right? I just came up with it."

"You're a genius."

"I know, right?" Her eyes sparkled when she smiled. "So. What time do you get to leave here?"

Janice said, "I can usually slip out between lunch and dinner. Four-thirty, five."

Lea took a card from the pocket of her jeans and held it out. "My studio. I'll spend today printing up some of our photos. Come by around then, and I can show you some of what I've put together."

"That sounds great. A-are you sure I can't pay you for all of this? You're doing so much work."

"I'm happy to do it."

Janice said, "In that case, you and Tori eat free here whenever you want. If I'm not here, just tell the waitress you're a friend."

"Not indefinitely," Lea said. "That would be far too much. A month, maybe."

"Two months."

"We can negotiate," Lea said.

Janice sighed. "Well, at least I can bring you dinner when I come to see the prints."

"Oh! That would definitely be a good reward."

Janice went to the hostess stand and came back with a menu.

"What are you going to have?" Lea asked as she skimmed the offerings.

"Oh, I didn't expect to-"

"You have to!" Lea said. "Please. It would be the perfect way to end the day. Looking over your art and then we could have dinner together. It's one of Tori's shift days, which means I will be eating alone otherwise. I might be used to eating alone, but I avoid it whenever possible."

Janice couldn't think of a way to refuse without sounding like she didn't want to have dinner with her. She wanted to. She definitely, absolutely wanted to. She couldn't even really say why she was trying to think of ways to say no. She didn't want to seem too eager? That was ridiculous. It was just dinner with a friend. A married friend. A married friend she had fucked twelve hours ago.

She tucked her hair behind her ears and blocked off all her second thoughts. "You know what, I don't like eating alone, either. I'll probably get one of the sandwiches. The chicken melt."

"Ooh," Lea said, skimming the menu. "Ooh! The ahi wrap! But without tomatoes."

"Those are delicious. Nothing compared to what you made for us last night, but still. You made a great choice."

Lea smiled and handed the menu back to her. "I can't wait." She held up her tablet. "I'll get back to the studio and get to work to earn the free meal. Around five?"

"Sounds good. I'll see you then."

Lea stepped in and hugged her. Janice returned the hug and breathed in the scent of Lea's perfume. Her brain fired with memories - their shower stall, the fogged-glass window, the caddy of body washes and shampoos - as she stepped back and tried to keep her face neutral.

When Lea was gone, Janice went back into the kitchen and made a note about what Lea had ordered. Evan drifted over to where she was and pointedly remained silent, arms crossed, staring hard at her as she wrote down the order, folded it, slipped it into her pocket, and turned her back on him.

"So much tension!" he said, following her.

"It's illegal for an employee to spy on their boss!" she said.

"I'm pretty sure it's the other way around. But go ahead, sue me." She went into her office. He leaned against the door frame. "So what's going to happen here?"

Janice looked behind him to make sure no one else was eavesdropping. "I'm not going to go into detail with you."

"No, I'm serious right now," he said. "I saw how you were with her. That was flirting."

"I wasn't~"

He held up a hand to stop her. "You're obviously going to keep being friends with them. I don't know either of them, but I kinda-sorta know you. And I've seen the way you are around both of them. You have to ask yourself if the..." He checked over his shoulder, double-checking the room. "If the thing that happened last night made things better or worse. Did it get things out of your system, or did it just lock things down hard?"

Janice shrugged. "It... helped. It was an outlet for whatever feelings of lust I had for them."

"Are you sure?" He pointed toward the dining room. "Because the person you became out there wasn't 'over it.' You looked like a teenager with a crush."

"Thank you for saying teenager."

He held up one hand. "It's not my place to say anything, obviously. But I know you don't have a lot of people in your life who know you well enough to say this. So it falls unto me. Threesomes can be a lot of fun. But they can also be horrible hand grenades. Especially when feelings get involved. You asked fire lady out on a date, and you spent a couple of days thinking she agreed and was interested. And then you met her wife, who is absolutely gorgeous and friendly and apparently a hugger. It would be easy to fall for either of them."

Janice shook her head. "We made an arrangement. It's going to happen again. So if I... get the urge, all I have to do is set it up."

"Uh-huh. So basically you're just a sentient sex toy sitting on the shelf until they're in the mood to play with you?"

"No!" She furrowed her brow. "No... that's not what it is. If I met someone... I would... It's just a fun distraction while I'm single. I have a free pass to sleep with two women I find very sexy, and I don't have to do the hard relationship stuff. It's win-win. The best of both worlds."

"While you're single," Evan repeated.

"Right."

"And you expect to find someone, fall for them, get into a committed relationship, while you're also casually banging a couple up in Uptown?"

"They don't live in Uptown."

"Well, wherever. I just don't want you to get hurt, and I want you to be happy. I don't think you'll be open to new possibilities if you're sitting around on-call with Mrs. and Mrs. Fire Lady. You deserve someone who looks at you the way you look at them. Don't be anyone's second choice."

Janice stared at him, surprised. "Wow, Evan. That was more serious than I think I've ever seen you."

"I can be serious." He mugged a comically serious expression. "When it matters, I can be serious." He pushed away from the door. "Just keep an eye on yourself. I have enough problems running your restaurant."

"You run the *kitchen*."

"Like there's a difference."

She shook her head and got up to close the door. She grudgingly admitted he had a point. It would be a hard thing to explain to any potential dates. *Yes, I'm sort of single, I mean there's this couple I've had sex with, but that's not like a serious relationship.* But she didn't have any prospects, didn't foresee much dating in her future, and she genuinely liked Tori and Lea. It might become an issue one day, if she happened to meet someone, but that was entirely hypothetical.

She wasn't going to deny herself a little, or a lot, a *hell of a lot* of fun in the meantime.

Janice made Lea's order herself and packaged it along with two bottles of Goose Island. She ignored Evan's look as she told him she was leaving the restaurant in his capable hands. She was already stressed and overthinking the entire situation thanks to their conversation earlier. She didn't need him adding to it with his mother-hen act.

Lea's studio was in one of the tall anonymous buildings in the Loop. Janice was surprised to discover it actually wasn't that far of a walk from the fountain where they had met just a couple of days ago. She marveled at how quickly the world could move as she crossed the lobby and took the elevator up to the eighth floor. The doors opened on a reception area so posh that for a second she assumed she had ended up on the wrong floor.

A woman in her twenties behind the polished black desk smiled at her, and Janice knew a meek retreat was out of the question.

"Hi," she said, stepping out of the elevator. "I'm looking for Contreras Studios."

"Of course. Do you have an appointment?"

Janice blanched. "She didn't mention I would need one. Um. I'm Janice Kozak..."

The girl's demeanor changed. "Oh! Yes, she mentioned you would be stopping by!" She stood up and took off her headset. "I'll take you right to her."

"Great," Janice said.

The girl smoothed her hands over her black pencil skirt and walked down the hall to the right. Janice followed, glancing at the offices she passed. Some led into waiting rooms, a few into empty offices, but everything was shining, gleaming, places that looked like she would have to pay a thousand dollar retainer just because she'd crossed the threshold.

At the end of the hall, the receptionist opened a door and leaned in. "Lea? Miss Kozak has arrived."

"Oh yay!" Lea's voice echoed from inside. "Thank you, Kathleen."

The receptionist, Kathleen, nodded and stepped aside. She folded her hands in front of her waist and smiled at Janice.

"Thank you."

"It's my pleasure," Kathleen said.

Janice went into the office, which turned out to be a large, stark space. The far side of the room had a plain white backdrop in place. Directly ahead of the entrance was a spiral staircase leading up to a second level which looked like it was playing host a half-dozen garage sales. She assumed everything there was a potential prop for photoshoots. But the neutrality of the room drew the eye to the real treasure in the room.

Beyond the stairs were three floor-to-ceiling windows that looked out over Lake Michigan, shining blue and perfect and stretching out to the horizon.

She wouldn't have thought they were high enough to see over the neighboring buildings, but this space seemed to have the perfect line of sight for maximum appeal.

Lea was suddenly next to her, and Janice laughed nervously. "Sorry. I'm probably the only person who has ever been distracted by this sight."

"Oh, yes, you're very strange. Most people don't even look over." She giggled and held out her hands, offering to take the to-go bag. "It smells wonderful! We can eat first, while it's fresh, and then I can show you how I spent the afternoon. You're going to love it."

Janice handed them over and followed Janice across the room to an open office.

"Lea... are you rich?"

Lea laughed and turned to look at her. "What?"

"Well..." She gestured around the studio. "When I saw the address was in the Loop, I thought the rent would have to be killing you. But look at this place! You have a second level, for crying out loud!"

"It's more of a loft," Lea said, looking up at the prop storage.

"A *loft*. And a receptionist!"

"She also covers a dentist, a tax accountant, and someone else who I can never remember." She thought for a second and then nodded her head to the side as if conceding a point someone else had made. "Sometimes she gets someone to cover the desk for a day so she can join me on a photoshoot as my assistant. But that's maybe once or twice a month. It's not like I have a full-time assistant or anything."

Janice laughed. "Splitting hairs! I'm sorry, but this place is ridiculous. I thought you were a freelance photographer. I-I pictured you taking pictures of kids' birthday parties and weddings."

"I do that sometimes, freelance. It makes sure I'm still having fun with the job, you know? Not so strict. Dealing with people instead of companies and products all the time, ugh." Lea altered her course from the office and went to another door. She opened it and stepped back to Janice could see inside. "But these are why I can afford this studio."

Inside, Janice saw what she could confidently describe as

photography supplies. But that was only because she had context clues. There were cameras, of course, and big vats that were currently empty, along with shelves of jugs and boxes with markings Janice couldn't decipher.

"I am not rich," Lea said. "My grandmother told me that if I made it through college, my reward would be greater than I ever imagined. I thought she was being metaphorical. But when I graduated, she told me about a bank account she'd opened when my parents got married. Every spare dime she had went into it. And by the time I graduated, it had grown large enough that I could buy all the best cameras, the best equipment, to be the best photographer possible. She said talent was vital, but the most talented birds still needed wings to fly. She wanted to give me wings."

"Wow."

Lea laughed softly. "The money just barely covered what I needed to get started. But it meant I could get really good jobs. Jobs that paid well. I work for magazines, fashion designers, I sometimes do celebrity portraiture..."

"Celebrities?"

Lea raised an eyebrow. "Mm-hmm. Maybe if you're good I will tell you some of their names."

"Any nudes...?" Janice asked.

"Oh yes." Lea said in a low voice, giving Janice a sultry look as she slid away and into her office. "We can eat in here, if you'd like."

Janice followed her into the office. "I'm sorry. I feel like I underestimated you. I thought I was doing you a favor, displaying your work in the restaurant. I thought it would be exposure." She laughed. "You definitely don't need any help in that department."

"Well, hopefully it will stop you from trying to pay me for the art. I can afford to spend some time on a project for a friend."

Lea cleared a place on her desk and gestured for Janice to sit across from her. "I've been thinking about this all day. When we left after that first night, I told Tori we'd have to keep going there until we'd eaten everything on the menu. I'll be one ahead of her."

"I'll have to buy her lunch sometime to keep things balanced."

"You should!" Lea chuckled. "Take her the chicken sandwich, though. She couldn't decide the other night, and that was the runner-up."

Janice said, "I'll keep it in mind."

They started eating. Lea snuck a glance at Janice and smirked, shaking her head. "I can't wait to show you the pictures. They turned out so good."

"I'm excited," Janice said. "We can also figure out a good day to have them delivered. O-or I can have someone come pick them up, or~"

Lea waved her off. "No, we can deliver, it's no problem."

Janice nodded and relaxed.

They were just friends having dinner together. She focused on that and, when her brain tried to run away again, she focused it on trying to think about the art. The shots had looked amazing on Lea's camera, so she could only imagine how they would look on the wall. By the time they moved on to the desserts Janice had packed - two servings of bread pudding, which Lea had never heard of and absolutely adored - she felt as if all the tension from how they'd spent the night before had vanished.

Given enough time, she could see herself settling into this new, odd friendship without suffering too much damage in the process.

Chapter Ten

LEA OPENED her eyes just after two in the morning without knowing what had woken her. She listened to the apartment and didn't hear anything unusual. The night sounds were typical of every other night. The hiss of the furnace, the sound of a door closing down the hall. And out in the city…

Sirens.

She sat up in bed and looked at the window, then retrieved her phone. The bright light stabbed her eyes, and she squeezed them shut for a moment before she tried looking again.

It had been a nice, quiet night until now. Dinner with Janice was fantastic. Great food and even better conversation. Janice had seemed a bit tense when she arrived, but her amazement at the studio had overpowered any nerves she'd been feeling. Lea had chuckled when she conveyed that part of the meeting to Tori on their bedtime phone call.

"She asked if I was rich."

"Well, you did spend a small fortune on that place," Tori said. "I don't blame her for being blown away by it."

"She was even more impressed by the pictures." Lea had made the call while lying in bed, shifting her legs under the blankets. She eyed the empty side of the mattress and remembered how full the bed had been the night before. "I think she wants to wallpaper the whole place with my work."

"I think she would be crazy not to," Tori said. "Your work is so beautiful."

"Thank you, baby," Lea said.

The rest of the conversation had been idle chat, talking just to hear the other person respond, and Lea kept it up until she couldn't keep her eyes open any longer. She said goodnight and plugged her phone into the charger with her last bit of energy.

Now, hours later and wide awake again, she couldn't remember if they'd said 'I love you' before hanging up. It wasn't a big deal. It happened. Tori would be called away by an alarm, Lea would get distracted by making dinner or film that needed tending. But for some reason tonight it seemed particularly important to remember if she'd remembered to say *te amo* before she disconnected the call. She thought she had. She was almost certain...

The sirens had faded, but that didn't help her anxiety about them. She sat up with her back against the headboard and opened the app Tori had told her to delete dozens of times. It provided a live feed of emergency radio broadcasts as a public service. She had Tori's station bookmarked.

"It does so much more harm than good," Tori had said when she found out Lea was using it.

"Not knowing does more harm," Lea argued. "The TV doesn't cover every fire, not even the internet does that, and I can't go back to sleep without knowing. So unless you want me to call you every time I hear a siren, I'm keeping it."

She clicked on Tori's station and closed her eyes. Ideally she would hear silence, just the hum of an empty line, but tonight she heard chatter.

"Engine 21 is on location." She recognized Conrad Weaver's voice and squeezed her eyes shut. Her heart was pounding. "Three story brick multi-residential structure, heavy smoke issuing from the second- and third-story windows on alpha side. Engine 21 will be laying a supply line and taking the handline to begin search and rescue operations. Engine 21 has command."

Dispatch acknowledged Conrad's report, but Lea had already stopped listening. The size-up was meant to give other responders an idea of what they would be facing when they arrived at the location. It also served to paint a pretty decent picture of what Tori was about to go into. She knew it was an apartment building, four floors, with a fire somewhere in the middle section.

Despite that, Lea couldn't help but picture the towering inferno. She squeezed her eyes shut and pulled her knees up to her chest, wrapped her arms around them, and listened as the chatter continued. She saw flames leaping up into the sky, lighting up the night. She saw doors exploding outward, floors collapsing, the building engulfed in bright flickering fire.

Hands shaking, she brought the phone up and closed the app. Her eyes stung, but she hadn't started crying yet. She dialed, and pressed the phone to her ear.

Two rings later, the phone stopped ringing and a muffled voice said, "M'lo...?"

"Janice?" The tears finally broke free.

"Lea?" She sounded more awake now. "What's wrong? Did something happen?"

"Can you come over?"

Janice had never ridden the train after midnight. She tried not to profile the two men and one woman in the car with her, but common sense forced her to keep an eye on them as she rode up to Addison. One man was standing directly in front of the doors, head down so that his face was almost touching the glass, but he immediately stepped out of the way at every stop in case anyone needed to get on or off. The other man had a blanket draped over his lap, and Janice tried very hard not to look in his direction. It was easier to assume he was just cold and not think about any other possibilities that way.

Part of her brain was still asleep. She barely remembered the phone call, had no idea how she had gotten dressed or what she was wearing. All she knew was that Lea had been crying and asked for her to come over. Odds were good it had something to do with Tori. That was enough for her. She had taken the time to check her phone for any emergency alerts, but there was nothing on any of the main news sites. She kept an eye out the window but if there were any fires, they weren't visible from the Red Line.

Lea and Tori lived relatively close to the station, so she didn't have to spend much time on the street. A few places were still open, lobbies brightly lit but completely empty. She heard cars she couldn't see, and the rumble of the train moving overhead on a neighboring block. It was like she'd slipped into a corner of the stage that wasn't needed for the scene, so the curtain had been drawn across it.

She was technically awake by the time she knocked on the apartment door. It swung open so quickly that she assumed Lea had been watching from the window. She wrapped Janice in a hug and pulled her inside.

"Thank you," Lea said quietly against Janice's shoulder. "I'm sorry. Thank you."

"Of course. How bad is it? I looked for smoke on the way over, but it's so dark..."

Lea sniffled and held up her phone. "It's on Southport, near the cemetery."

"Okay." Janice guided her to the couch and sat down with her. "But how bad is it? Is it multiple buildings, are there other fire departments there..."

"Oh." Lea wiped the back of her hand across her eyes. "Uh. It's out."

Janice furrowed her brow. "It's out?"

"Well, it's not out. An apartment building caught fire. But i-it's contained. They're stopping it from spreading." She took a deep breath and shook her head. "Oh my god. I made you come all the way out here in the middle of the night for nothing. I'm so sorry."

"Don't be sorry." Janice put a hand on Lea's shoulder and squeezed. "You didn't know how bad it was at the time. I can't imagine how that uncertainty would feel."

Lea made a face that looked almost angry. "Well. No. I knew."

"What?"

"The app I use." She held up her phone again. "I can listen to their radio broadcasts. They do a size-up of the fire when they arrive and they keep dispatch informed about the progress, so I knew... I knew it was a small one. I knew when I called and asked you to come."

Janice was confused. "Then why..." The answer hit her before she had even figured out what she was going to ask. "This happens with every fire, doesn't it? That's why you reacted the way you did when you heard sirens the other day."

"I've tried." Lea was crying again. "I went to therapy for two years when we first got together. And I tried again for a year after we got married. But I couldn't... figure it out. I didn't know what getting better looked like. Because it felt like I was looking for tricks to not worry about my wife. The woman I loved had a job where she goes into burning buildings. And it doesn't matter how good she is, there's always a chance she'll... it will..."

She pressed her lips together and twisted to face Janice again. She put her head down on Janice's shoulder.

"I'm sorry I dragged you all the way out here."

Janice put her arms around Lea. "Don't be. It sounds like you needed someone here."

"God." Lea wiped at her face. "I-I want to say you don't have to stay here. But also, I can't just send you back out. Did you take the train?"

"Yeah..."

"No," Lea slumped. "I'm sorry. I'm stupid, I'm~"

"No, no." She hugged Lea tighter, moving a hand into her hair. "I want to be here."

"Thank you, Rico."

Janice laughed. "If I have to have a nickname, I want one for you, too."

"We'll find one. Maybe we'll ask Tori to come up with it." She sat up. "We should try to get some sleep. I think I can relax now that I have someone here with me."

"Okay. If you're sure."

"Mm-hmm. They probably won't be updating much, and the news won't cover it until the morning edition, if they even bother with a story. No point in staying awake waiting."

Janice nodded. "Okay, then."

Lea stood and held out her hand. "Come on."

"Oh. I'm, I think... I'm fine on the couch."

"Don't be silly. We slept together last night."

Janice smiled. "Yeah. But we also *slept together* last night. And Tori was there. It was a different situation. I don't know if I would feel right about it."

Lea sat down again. "It would just be sleeping."

"I know. Even then, it seems like something we should talk over with Tori."

"I suppose you're right... No. You're absolutely right."

Janice watched Lea's face, noted the way her voice trailed off. She cupped Lea's face and made her look up.

"You really won't be able to sleep unless someone is with you."

"No, no." Lea pulled back and stood up. "It's fine. You can take the couch. It will be close enough."

Janice stood up. "Come on."

"No, it's okay, really. If you're not comfortable~"

"Sh. You heard Tori this morning, right? She's not going to get jealous over a good-morning kiss, and I don't think she'd get upset about providing comfort when it's needed."

Lea chewed her lip, conflicted, but then she took Janice's hand. "It's just sleeping."

"Right. So come on. It's late, and we both need to get some sleep."

Lea nodded and guided Janice to the bedroom.

Tori could barely keep her eyes open for the drive home. She was sore, frustrated, exhausted, and she could smell herself to an upsetting degree. She'd barely gotten to sleep when the alarm came. She'd left her cozy bed to walk through an apartment building filled with more smoke than oxygen to make sure everyone was out, then greeted the sunrise by hanging around outside securing the building and assessing the damage.

She parked and climbed the stairs to their apartment, already fantasizing about the six or seven hours of sleep ahead of her.

"Lea, *estoy aquí*." She put down her coat and bag, then went into the kitchen to start Lea's coffee. She heard the bedroom door open while she was pouring her orange juice. "*Buenos...*" She cut herself off when she realized the woman sheepishly coming down the hall was not Lea, but Janice. Her hair was a mess and she was wearing clothes that were clearly pajamas. She looked like she anticipated a fight.

"Good morning," Tori said cautiously.

"Hi," Janice said. "We... we slept. We just slept. We were going to send you a text, just to make sure everyone was... in the loop. But she fell asleep so fast. And I didn't have your number, and I didn't feel right using her phone, so I thought if she woke up before you got home, we..." She scratched her neck and looked toward the window. "Gosh. Wow. This looks bad."

Tori carefully closed the juice and put it back in the fridge. In her mind, she knew that Lea and Janice had spent a lot of time together while she was at work. Dinner at the studio and everything. But she also knew Lea had been alone when she went to bed. And the biggest piece of evidence that nothing happened was the T-shirt Janice was wearing.

"I've never seen that shirt," Tori said.

"What?" Janice looked down at herself. It was a yellow T-shirt with the Wrigley marquee with the words No Lights In Wrigley in place of the park name. It was faded and stretched out from dozens of washings. She looked up again, confused. "You haven't? I know it's old, but..."

"I mean I've never seen it here, which means it isn't mine. Or Lea's. Which means you put it on at home. Which means you came over here sometime after you were already in bed." She kept her voice steady. "She called you, didn't she."

Janice swallowed. "I don't know why, but I get the feeling you're not mad at me anymore."

Tori shook her head. "I'm not mad. But you should probably go."

"Yeah, that's..." She moved quickly to the couch and retrieved her shoes. "Lea is still asleep. I got out of bed without waking her. God, that sounds... We just slept. We really just slept."

"I know. And for what it's worth, I'm glad you were here for her."

Janice relaxed a little. "She was hysterical. Panicking."

Tori nodded. "I know. For the record, this doesn't change anything about..." She waved her hand. "Anything. Us, the three of us. That's all still good."

"Oh." Fear and relief washed over her face. She clearly hadn't even considered that. "Oh, good. I'll, um." Janice hesitated. "W-well, you know where to find me."

Tori nodded again, and Janice fled.

Once she was gone, Tori finished her juice and went into the bedroom. Lea was curled around the pillow, hair across her face like an eye mask, her knees bent as if she'd just fallen down while running. Tori went to her side of the bed and sat down, resting her back against the headboard.

A few minutes later, Lea breathed in deeply and stretched. She lifted her head without opening her eyes and muttered Tori's name. She scooted closer, sliding her hand over Tori's thigh to situate herself before she moved down to lay her head in her wife's lap. Then realization hit her and she opened her eyes, looked up at Tori, and scanned the room.

"Janice already left," Tori said.

"We only~"

"You only slept. She said. I know." She let Lea sit up. "You lied to me."

"No, she didn't come over~"

Tori shook her head. "Not about *that*. I don't care about her being here. I'm glad she was here for you. You lied about therapy."

Lea repositioned herself so that she was also leaning against the headboard. "I tried. But I kept thinking that if it was successful, I would... what? Care less about you? Fuck that."

Tori sighed. "It's not about how much you care. It's about managing your fear and anxiety~"

"What if I'm lying here asleep and something happens to you? What if me being awake and, and sending my concern out into the universe~"

"Please don't start with that, Lea." She closed her eyes and rocked her head back. "I'm so exhausted."

Lea crossed her arms. "It's a superstition, okay? I understand that. And I'm okay with it. I decided it was something I could live with, and I've been doing it. Every shift, every call you've gone out on. I've paced and stayed up~"

"Every~" Tori opened her eyes. "Give me your phone."

Lea realized her mistake. "No."

"Lea, you said you deleted that fucking app."

"I did. And the only thing worse than knowing is having no way to check."

"Damn it, Lea." She got out of bed and walked to the wall. "Am I supposed to just be okay with this? Do you think it's easy for me going into burning buildings knowing what might happen? Knowing you're back here eavesdropping on Conrad's updates? We all have people at home waiting for us, worried for us. But we have to block that out so we can do the job."

Lea drew her knees up to her chest and wrapped her arms around them. "I guess I'm not as strong as you."

Tori walked back to the bed. "That's why there are support groups. Other wives you can talk to, confide in, worry with."

"I don't know them." She hugged her legs tighter. "Janice helped. Having her here helped."

Tori relaxed slightly. "Really? You're not just saying that?"

"No. She calmed me down. And I... I liked being held. I swear to you, nothing sexual happened."

"I know," Tori said softly.

Lea narrowed her eyes. "Oh. Maybe that's worse. Emotional cheating."

"No," Tori said. "You needed someone. It couldn't be me, so it had to be someone else. I'm glad it was someone I also like. I really mean that. I'm not jealous of her."

She sat down on the mattress. After a moment, Lea crawled to her, hugged her from behind, and kissed her neck.

"I'm sorry I lied to you. About therapy. And the app."

Tori covered Lea's hands, then twisted and kissed her lips. "I love you."

"I love you, too. I really am sorry."

"I know, *querida*." She brought Lea's hand up to her mouth and kissed the knuckles. A thought occurred to her, and she tilted her head to the side. "The fire was at two in the morning. What time did you call Janice?"

Lea shrugged. "Around then. Maybe two-thirty." She pulled away from Tori and walked on her knees toward the nightstand. "I can check my phone."

Tori said, "And she came?"

"Mm-hmm." Lea realized what Tori was getting at. "Yes. I didn't even have to tell her what was wrong. She just heard that I was upset and she came."

"At two-thirty in the morning."

"Two thirty-three," Lea said, holding up the call log.

Tori looked at her. "Huh. That's something worth thinking about..."

Lea raised an eyebrow and nodded.

CHAPTER ELEVEN

THAT AFTERNOON, once Tori had gotten a few hours of sleep, she woke up to an empty apartment. Lea was at the studio and would probably be there until dinner. So Tori dressed and headed for Canvas.

Tori requested to be sat at the same table she and Lea had been given on their first visit. She skimmed the menu, sipped her water, and eyed the walls to see where the art Lea was working on would go. She had ordered by the time Janice came out of the kitchen. She looked like she was anticipating an execution, so Tori offered a smile and gestured at the seat across from her.

"If it's okay," Tori said, "I want to talk before you say anything."

Janice nodded.

"Good. I wanted to say thank you, sincerely, for coming when Lea called last night. This morning. Whatever. Her anxiety over my job has been an issue for a while. I thought she had a handle on it, but it turns out she's been lying to me about it. That's why I was angry this morning. It had nothing to do with you, or the fact you were there."

The tension faded from Janice's shoulders. "Thank God. I~"

"I'm not done."

Janice pressed her lips together. Tori leaned forward.

"I think you're falling in love with my wife."

Tori's eyes widened. "I know I'm not supposed to talk, but I barely know her. We've spent a couple of hours together. Some of those hours were... much, much better than others, granted~"

"I think Lea is falling in love with you, too."

That shut Janice up. "I think I should let you talk."

Tori looked around to make sure no one was close enough to listen in. "I know Lea. I know how she acts around people, and I can tell that she has feelings for you. You know that saying, 'where there's smoke, there's fire'? And yes, the firefighter is making a fire analogy..."

Janice chuckled nervously.

"You being in the apartment this morning? That was smoke. Lea has been dealing with these anxiety attacks alone for six years, and this is the first time she's called anyone to be there with her. I should be jealous. But I'm just happy she wasn't alone. And like you said, I might not know you very well, but I know that when Lea called you at two-thirty, you rode the train across town to be there for her. How many of your friends would you have done that for?"

"Not a lot."

"No, I didn't think so. More smoke. That's enough for me to assume something is burning somewhere."

Janice rubbed her hands together. "I'm not a homewrecker. I'm... I'm not sure how I feel about Lea. I like her. I like her a lot. And I like you. But regardless of what those feelings might be, I would never break up a marriage."

Tori shook her head. "I'm not worried about that. I never said I thought Lea was falling out of love with me, or shifting her affections, or anything like that. I think she loves us both."

Janice's eyebrows twitched, betraying her confusion.

Tori wet her lips. "The problem here is us. You and me. Other than an initial attraction and the night we had together, we haven't gotten to know each other the way you and Lea have."

"Okay," Janice said slowly.

"I'm here to ask you out."

Janice blinked. "On a date?"

"On a... day." She gestured toward the windows. "Like you and Lea had. You walked around downtown. You had dinner at her studio. You spent quality time together, just the two of you. I'd like for us to have the same opportunity to bond."

For a while, Janice didn't say anything. She looked down at the table, worked her lips, searched the room for clues, all while flipping through a series of responses in her head. Finally she looked at Tori again.

"What did you have in mind?"

"A baseball game," Tori said. "A guy I work with has season tickets. I can wrangle a couple from him. I thought maybe you liked baseball because of the, you know, the Cubs shirt you were wearing this morning."

"Oh. Right. Yeah. I-I like baseball."

Tori nodded. "Okay. We can figure out everything else later on. But I can text you when I find out the specifics of what tickets I can get."

"Sounds... good." Janice wet her lips. "What's... what's..." She made a gesture with her hand. "I don't want to say 'what's the point', but really, wh-why are you bothering to go to all this trouble? Why are we going on a date if you're already married? If you think your wife and I are falling in love with each other. Shouldn't you want to keep us as far apart as possible? I mean, that's *my* instinct."

"Because I like that you care about Lea. I like that she had someone she could call when she was hurting, and that person cared enough to risk going out in the middle of the night just to hold her. You didn't ask for anything in return, you just sat with her. I think Lea needs that. And it's something I can't give her. So if you... and I... if *we* all agree that we fit together, and work well together, then maybe what we did the other night can be more than just a... fun thing we do sometimes."

"Are you inviting me into your marriage?" Janice's voice was so low Tori could barely hear it.

Tori shrugged. "Right now I'm inviting you to a baseball game. From there? Who knows."

Captain Gambol was willing to sacrifice tickets for the next home game against Cincinnati. She offered to pay face value, but he waved her off. "They would've gone to waste anyway. Take 'em. Try to have fun knowing that you will owe me. One huge favor. That you can't refuse."

"Be careful, Captain," she said. "I could construe that as sexual harassment."

"True. But you know that I am very much in love with my wife, and would much rather have you... oh, I don't know... man the grill at my next barbeque."

Tori shook her head. "I should never have let you taste my ribs."

Gambol grinned, his teeth shining under his mustache. "Out of context, *that* sounds like harassment. Very, very weird harassment."

"I don't know any other kind," Tori said.

She texted Janice to make sure the day of the game worked for her - it did - and went back to work. She was able to put the whole endeavor out of her mind until that weekend. She started getting ready and realized she felt the same nerves and anxiety she used to get when she went on dates. It seemed wholly unfair that she was suffering them again.

"Maybe I should have gotten three tickets," Tori said, using the bathroom mirror to figure out what her hair was capable of doing.

Lea, sitting on the bed to enjoy the spectacle of her wife's preparations, smiled. "The whole point of this is for you and Janice to spend some time together. Without me."

Tori sighed. "I just like a buffer."

"I know, baby." She sat up and put her feet on the floor. "We can probably get a last minute ticket if you're really feeling anxious."

"No," Tori said reluctantly. "You're right, this is about seeing how we click. Besides, it wouldn't be as fun with you there."

Lea's jaw dropped. "How. *Dare*. You."

"C'mon, honey. You know it's true. You don't even like baseball."

"I..." She hunched her shoulders. "I don't... hate it. I know the big players. Mickey Mantle, Satchel Paige, Caroline Rainy."

Tori smiled. "Can you name one from this century?"

"Those weren't from this century?" Lea got off the bed and went to Tori. She turned her around and reached up to tease her hair. "You are an amazing woman, okay? You're fascinating, you're fun, and being around you is joyous. You have nothing to worry about. Remember, all this started because *she* asked *you* out on a date. She was interested from the first moment."

"I guess. I just feel like I'm starting from behind and playing catch-up."

"It isn't a game." She straightened Tori's collar and smoothed down wrinkles on the shoulders. "You just have to find out if you like her. And if she likes you. Which she will. And I think you will like her, too. She's very great."

Tori nodded and put her hands on Lea's hips. "And what if we click? What if I decide I like her as much as you do?"

Lea looked into Tori's eyes. "Then we work out everything else and move forward from there." She took a step back and examined Tori's outfit. She nodded her approval. "So go over your plans one more time. It will ease your mind."

Tori sighed. "We meet at Wrigley. We watch the game, which should end around eight-thirty. Then we go out for dinner. And then back here to give you a full report."

"Okay..."

"What?"

"No, I'm just... thinking. When she came over the other night, we talked about spending the night together without you knowing or giving permission. It made sense to me that you should have had a say in what happened that night. And even though you were more angry about my lying to you, I think there's a part of you that also wishes we had told you before it happened."

Tori shrugged. "Well, you *are* my wife. I would've liked to get a heads-up before I found another woman coming out of our bedroom. Even though our circumstances were a little weird."

"Right. So to avoid that happening tonight, I wanted to be clear." She cleared her throat. "You can kiss her if the moment arises."

"Okay."

"You can go home with her."

Tori frowned. "Really?"

"Mm-hmm," Lea said. "This is about chemistry, right? Figuring out how you feel about her. Sex is a part of that. If the moment strikes, and if she invites you..."

"But you're here. Why wouldn't we just come here and~"

"Because tonight isn't about me and Janice, or the three of us together. We already know that I have feelings for Janice. We need to find out how you feel about each other. If you have feelings that are, I don't know, seventy percent physical, then we need to know that."

Tori nodded, still uncertain. "Okay. If it comes up, I'll keep it in mind. But what about the opposite situation? What if we go to the game and discover we have nothing in common, nothing to talk about, can't stand each other's company..."

"I don't think that will happen."

"But what if it does?"

Lea thought for a second and then shook her head. "Then I

won't call her again. I have feelings for her, yes, but it's a crush. Yes, there's a potential for it to get bigger, but it's only been two weeks since we met. Two weeks! If I stop seeing her, the feelings will go away."

"I'm not sure I want them to go away. I want her to be there for you."

"We'll figure something out." She stepped closer and put her hands on Tori's cheeks, guiding her down for a kiss. "Nothing you're uncomfortable with. Don't force anything with her. Just be natural, be yourself, and focus on enjoying the night. Don't think of what it might mean. Okay?"

Tori nodded. "I'll try. *Te amo.*"

"*Te amo.*" She kissed Tori again and stepped away from her. "You look gorgeous. Go. Enjoy yourself."

"I'll try. But it will be hard to top the last date I went on."

Lea grinned. "Flirt. Text me when the game is over so I'll know whether or not to wait up."

"Which one are you rooting for?"

"Honestly?" Lea said. "Neither. Whatever happens, happens. I'm just excited about the possibilities."

Tori took a breath and let it out slowly. She had to admit, even with the nerves, she was just as excited. She decided to use Lea's words to keep herself from worrying too much.

Whatever happens, happens. They would figure out the next step later, together.

Janice rubbed her hands together even though she wasn't cold, pacing in front of the park's famous marquee. Groups of people moved past and around her on their way inside, but she refused to check the time. She knew she was early. And if Tori was running a little late, well, that was to be expected. Even though she lived walking distance from the park, so traffic wasn't an issue.

She pulled her phone out and checked for any missed calls or messages.

Maybe it was a good sign. Or at least a hopeful one. Maybe Tori was feeling the same anxiety that had been weighing on Janice's mind since they locked in the details of their date.

And it was a date. Right? They were exploring their compatibility. Seeing if they had the same chemistry Janice had with Lea. And if the answer was yes... But if the answer was no...? She didn't know how to branch out from either of those questions. So she had spent as much time at work as possible, fully focused on the restaurant so she would be exhausted by the time she got home. Work and sleep. She even took her phone into the bathroom when she showered so she could blast music to prevent her mind from wandering.

The day before, Lea's studio had delivered the photographs to the restaurant. Janice had been nervous about seeing Lea again, but they'd arrived with two strong young men and a woman who introduced herself as the studio's "installation consultant." She was relieved to avoid any uncomfortable conversations but, at the same time, disappointed. She hadn't seen Lea since the night of the phone call. They had texted a few times but it seemed best to take a little space ahead of her evening with Tori. A palate cleanser, of sorts.

She continued pacing. When she looked south, she saw someone walking on the opposite side of the street. She was wearing a denim coat with the collar flipped up to reveal the fleece lining. *That's her*, Janice thought, followed immediately by, *wait, no it isn't*. Then the woman crossed the street and Janice's heart leapt into her throat.

Oh. It is her. That's her.

It was strange to see someone transform from a random passerby to a person she cared about. She almost felt the shift in her mind, like a pair of glasses had been dropped down over her eyes and suddenly part of the scenery had magically come to life.

"Hi," Tori said. "I hope you weren't waiting too long."

"No, not at all." Honestly Janice couldn't have said exactly how long she'd been there. "You're worth waiting for. You look great."

"Oh thanks." Tori looked down at herself as if she'd forgotten what she had on. She nodded at the main entrance of the park. "Should we go in?"

"Sure, yeah."

As they joined the crowd, Janice asked, "So how's Lea doing?"

"She's doing well. She..." Janice could tell she almost said one thing, then took a pause in order to say something else. "She hasn't had any really rough nights like the one you saw. Just so you won't be worried about getting a call every time I'm on duty."

"Tell her I wouldn't mind. If she needs someone, I'm happy to lend a shoulder."

"She knows. But I'll pass it along. It's... it can be hard to ask for help in moments like that. People think 'it's not her problem, it's mine, I shouldn't bother her with it.' I know that you mean it when you say you want to be there for her. I'll make sure she really understands."

"Good. It's nice to be needed."

"Definitely." Tori glanced at the concession stands. "I know we're going to have dinner after this, but that's going to be in, like, three hours. Do you want something to eat? There's pretzels, hot dogs, burgers... we could probably get enough food here to count as dinner."

"No, I'm fine right now," Janice said. "Check in again after a few innings, though."

Janice smiled. "Will do."

The seats were in the last row of the Field Box, along the first baseline. They settled into their seats and Janice looked out over the field. The players of both teams were warming up. The sun was already starting to set and the flood lights were turned on. Janice nudged Tori and pointed up at the lights.

"Did you know Wrigley was the last major league park to have night games?"

"Yeah. I saw your T-shirt, remember?"

Janice smiled. "A lot of people in this neighborhood *hated* the idea. They thought drunks would be roaming the streets. But in 2016, all the World Series home games were played at night. So some people think that putting in the lights broke the curse."

"Huh. Does the shirt indicate where you stand on that theory?"

"No, that was just something I picked up at a thrift shop when I first got to town. I bought all kinds of kitschy Chicago stuff to... I don't know, remind me where I was when I woke up in the morning. Even after all this time I don't really feel a hundred percent acclimated."

Tori nodded. "It can take some time, especially if you had strong roots where you came from. We won't treat you like an outsider. Just as long as you don't put ketchup on your hot dogs."

Janice laughed and turned to face her. "Yeah, okay, what is the deal with that?"

"Because you're not ordering a *hot dog*. You're ordering a Chicago dog, and a true Chicago dog has mustard, pickles, relish, onions, tomatoes, and peppers. There's no room there for ketchup. It changes the whole chemical makeup of the dog. Besides, you have the tomatoes. Adding ketchup is redundant. You put ketchup on it, and that could be from New York or LA or Seattle, but it is *not* from

Chicago."

"I'm convinced!" Janice laughed. "I promise I'll try one."

Tori looked at her. "You've lived here a year and a half and you haven't had a hot dog?"

"I'm not really a~ oh."

Tori was already up. She turned around, stepped on her seat, and threw her leg over the railing to climb out onto the walkway. Janice watched the whole process, treated to a perfect angle of the seat of Tori's jeans.

"I'll be right back," Tori said, already jogging away. "Beer to drink?"

"Uh yeah, sure..."

Janice watched her go, then faced the field again. She looked around at the other people in their section. She felt the crowd size was just right. Not too many people, but the park didn't seem abandoned. She shifted her focus to the players and tried to read the names on the jerseys. She really was a baseball fan, but a relatively new one. Moving to Chicago, it had seemed like a rite of passage to at least be aware of the Cubs.

She was starting to wonder if Tori had ditched her when a hand holding a hot dog appeared over her left shoulder. She jumped, laughed, and took the offered snack. Tori climbed back over the railing and dropped down into her seat, arranging her own food on her lap. She was wearing two baseball caps. She took off the top one and gently laid it on Janice's head.

"I bought you a souvenir."

"Thank you very much." Janice adjusted the hat, placing it so it would stay. She examined the hot dog carefully. "It does look like... a... very specific thing."

Tori laughed. "Yes. If you don't like it, I can go get you something else."

"You'd just come back with a deep-dish pizza."

Tori laughed harder. "It would serve you right." She held up her beer bottle. "Enjoy."

Janice tapped the neck of her bottle against Tori's. Then she put the beer down so she could use both hands on the hot dog. She figured out how to lift it with the least amount of spillage.

Tori turned to someone seated near them. "It's her first Chicago dog."

Janice cringed. "Oh god, now I'm a spectacle..."

"Put on a happy face," Tori said. We don't want a riot on our hands."

Janice took a breath, let it out, and then took a bite. She chewed slowly, her eyes on the field to ignore the eyes of the people around her. She swallowed, licked her lips, and then took a drink of her beer. Finally, once her mouth was empty again, she held out her hand with the thumb raised.

Tori led their neighbors in the first cheer of the game.

CHAPTER TWELVE

BY THE seventh inning, Janice was hungry enough to decide eating at the park would work as dinner.

"Not that I'm trying to cut the night short or anything."

"No, I understand," Tori said, moving her beer to the cup holder to stand. "I'm pretty hungry myself. What do you feel like?"

Janice stood up with her. "Let's go together. I can see what looks appealing."

Tori climbed over the railing, then helped Janice get over it as well.

"Between you and Lea, I'm getting a real authentic Chicago experience. She showed me the art, the trains, the hidden gems. And now you've treated me to a Cubs game and a true authentic hot dog. Thank you for being such good tour guides."

"We're just being good neighbors. I'm glad we got to you before you tried to ask for ketchup at a hot dog stand. You might've gotten thrown in the lake."

Janice laughed. "Bullet dodged. Anything else I need to know?"

"Hm. I don't think so. You already lived through a winter, so that won't be a surprise. I think you're good until St. Patrick's Day."

"Green river."

"Yep," Tori said.

"So. We'll, um, still be hanging out together in March?"

Tori reached out and took Janice's hand. She laced their fingers together and bumped her arm against Janice's shoulder.

"Yeah. I think we will."

Janice grinned and leaned against Tori's side as they continued their search for dinner.

Lea was sitting up in bed reading when Tori got home. She had planned on going to bed early, so she wouldn't think about what was happening a few blocks away at Wrigley. Originally she'd found a broadcast of the game, but she shut it off because she analyzed every sound from the crowd in a futile attempt to pinpoint Tori or Janice. But sleep hadn't been possible, either. Trying to ignore their date only moved it centerstage of her mind and shined a big spotlight on it.

So she tucked herself in with a book of Seattle photos and paged through it, hoping to make her eyes tired enough that they bypassed her brain and put her to sleep.

It was a little past nine-thirty when she heard the front door open and close. She jumped, dropped the book, and kicked her legs to free them from the blanket.

"Baby?" she called. "I'm in here."

She had just stood up when Tori came into the bedroom. She shrugged out of her coat as she crossed the room, letting it fall to the floor. A baseball cap she hadn't been wearing when she left also fell, but Lea was more concerned about the intense look in her wife's eye.

"Tori...?"

Tori grabbed her, kissed her hard, and pushed her back onto the bed. Lea yelped and grabbed two handfuls of Tori's shirt as she was dropped onto the mattress. Tori settled on top of her, kissing her lips hard before moving down to her neck.

"Wait, wait, wait," Lea said, laughing breathlessly. "Tell me how tonight went."

Tori sat up. "I like her. I like her a lot." She kissed Lea's lips again and settled between her legs.

Lea twisted out of the kiss and moved her mouth to Tori's ear. She bit down on the lobe just hard enough to make Tori tense in her arms.

"Tell me about tonight. I want to know everything." She licked the spot she had just bitten.

"I got her a Chicago-style hot dog. Her first." Tori pushed

herself up on her knees. She put her hands on Lea's shoulders, then dragged them down over her breasts, cupping them through her shirt. "I told her why she couldn't have ketchup on it."

Lea giggled. "Good, good. What else?"

"We talked for most of the game. About Seattle. About starting the restaurant." She pushed up Lea's shirt and brushed her fingertips over her stomach. Her fingers were cold, but Lea didn't mind. She put her arms over her head and watched, twitching when Tori's hands reached the waistband of her pants. "She's funny," Tori said. "She laughs at my stupid jokes."

"Your jokes are hilarious."

Tori unbuttoned her pants. Lea lifted her hips to help her drag them down.

"After the game..." Tori lifted Lea's right leg and kissed the ankle. "I walked her to the train. It felt like a real date. I told her that I had your permission to kiss her goodnight."

Lea drew in a breath. "Did you kiss her?"

"I did." Tori kissed down Lea's leg. "I kissed her softly, and she kissed me back like she wanted it to go further. And I wanted it too."

She moved higher, brushed her cheek over Lea's hip. Lea was breaking out in goosebumps all over, both from the story and from Tori's soft touches. She imagined them standing on the street, in the darkness beneath the L tracks. Tori bending down to kiss her, Janice stretching up to meet her, their lips meeting and then crushing together...

"Come here." Lea was still trying to catch her breath. "Come here, please, please. Kiss me."

Tori slid up Lea's body and kissed her. Lea reached between them and unbuttoned Tori's pants. She pushed them down just enough to get her hand between her legs. Tori shifted her weight and pressed one thigh against Lea's sex. Lea ran her free hand up under Tori's shirt, while Tori's hands were free to explore Lea's body. Lea pushed down against Tori's thigh as her fingers pulled aside the cotton underwear and massaged the skin underneath.

"You're wet," she whispered against Tori's mouth.

"She asked me to go home with her," Tori said.

Lea inhaled sharply. "She wanted you."

"She wanted me to fuck her."

Lea whimpered and arched her back. "I said you could, baby..."

"I know." Tori thrust against Lea, her hands now on her hips, guiding her, keeping her in place. "I told her..." Lea's fingers were suddenly inside her, and Tori's voice momentarily stopped working. "I told her I thought... it was best... if we sealed our arrangement together. Not... not just..."

"That makes sense," Lea groaned.

"Then I bent down and whispered in her ear."

Lea whimpered.

"I told her I was going to come home and fuck you."

Lea squirmed and squeezed her legs around Tori's. "Please..."

"I told her..." For a few seconds, the only sounds Tori could make were incoherent. Then she regained her composure. "I told her... you would call her after you came."

"Victoria..."

"Come for me, Lea. Janice is waiting."

Lea squeezed her eyes shut and clung to Tori, trembling through her orgasm, lifting her hips to grind down on Tori's thigh. She had two fingers inside Tori and felt her coming, too, and they rocked against each other and made quiet, incoherent sounds of pleasure. Tori went limp first, dropping her weight onto Lea's chest before she pushed up and rolled to the side.

They stared at the ceiling as they caught their breath. Lea dropped her hand down and blindly groped for Tori's, squeezing the fingers when she finally found it.

"Phone?"

"Hm? Oh." Tori's pants were still around her thighs. She reached down with her free hand, pulled the phone from her pocket, and handed it to Lea.

"You really told her I'd call?"

"I did."

Lea smiled and opened the contacts. "You should have called her before you came in. Put it on speaker. Let her listen to it on the train."

"That would have been cruel," Tori said, laughing. "Next time, maybe."

"Mm-hmm," Lea said, putting her phone to her ear. It buzzed with a ring tone. Lea lifted Tori's hand, looked at their interlaced fingers, and guided Tori's hand to her crotch.

Janice answered. "Lea?"

"Hello, Janice."

She gave a surprised, breathy laugh. "I can't believe you're actually calling."

"Well, she did promise." She put her hand flat on top of Tori's. "Thank you. You got her so riled up that she attacked me as soon as she walked in the door. Threw me down on the bed. Yanked my pants down. She pressed her thigh against me. I put my fingers in her."

Janice's breathing was rough. "Shit. I-I'm still on the street. Walking down the street."

"How far are you from home?"

"I'm at the corner."

Lea licked her lips and closed her eyes. "Tori is rubbing my pussy right now."

"Oh God. You two are fucking evil."

Lea smiled. "Hurry home, Miss Kozak. We'd love for you to join in the fun."

Tori rolled onto her side and leaned in so that her lips were right above Lea's. "Don't let her tease you, Janice." She pressed a kiss to Lea's mouth. "I'm not going to let her come until you do."

Lea whined, "No!"

"You deserve it for being a brat," Tori said softly, still rubbing.

Janice was panting now. Lea assumed she was jogging. "I don't know how much longer..."

"Wait, wait, wait."

Tori said, "We're waiting, Janice. She's right on the edge. I can tell."

Lea heard the sound of footsteps on stairs. "Hurry," she sighed. "Please." The jingle of keys, and then a door slammed. She heard Janice swearing under her breath.

"Oh god. Oh god, okay... fuck..."

Tori turned her head slightly toward the phone. "Are you taking your clothes off for us, Janice?"

"Yes..."

"Good girl," Lea purred, writhing against Tori's hand, which had regained its earlier energy.

Janice said, "I'm touching myself." She sighed, sounding relieved. "Oh fuck, you two are so sexy... Make her come, Tori."

Lea tightened her grip on Tori's arm. "Please, Rico, please."

Janice cried out on the other end of the line, and Lea came for the second time that night, bending her knees so that her feet rose into the air. She bucked against Tori's hand, then pinned it between her thighs and rolled to face her. She buried her face in Tori's shirt, burrowing against her. Tori kept the phone lifted so they could both hear Janice's heavy breathing.

"Holy shit," Janice finally said.

"Where are you?" Tori asked.

"Right inside my apartment." She exhaled sharply. "I literally dropped everything and leaned against the door. Really hoping none of my neighbors were walking by in the past few minutes."

Tori said, "Lea is curled up against me. It's adorable."

"I wish I could see her."

"Me too," Tori said.

Lea had her eyes closed, listening to their voices as her body stopped singing. Her sensitivity levels eventually dropped out of the red, and she was able to relax and cuddle up against Tori. She lifted her head.

"Thank you, Janice. For the call, and for tonight."

"I feel weird taking gratitude for it. I had a great night. I had a hot dog. Tori bought me a hat. I almost had to masturbate in the lobby of my building. Definitely a good evening. So... good night."

"Good night, Janice," Tori said.

Lea said, "Good night, Rico." She disconnected the call and lifted her eyes to Tori. "So what happens now?"

"Now I think we all need to calm down," Tori said. "And get some sleep. Then... dinner? We can talk this out face to face now that we have a better idea of where we all stand."

"Just to say it out loud," Lea said, pushing herself up on one elbow. "I love you, Victoria. I love you very much. And I also have very strong feelings for Janice, and I would like to explore them."

Silence from Janice's end. Lea was about to prompt her when she finally spoke. "I have feelings for both of you. I didn't plan on it. But spending time with you separately, and spending time with you together, I just... at the end of the day... I just want more."

Lea looked at Tori, still nervous of what she would say, but relief washed over her when she saw the small, beautiful smile on her lips.

"I want more, too," Tori said. "I love Lea. And I have feelings for you, Janice. And I think I'd like to see where it goes."

Lea grinned, her heart soaring as she rolled on top of Tori.

Janice sat with her back against the door of her apartment, jeans around her thighs. She was pressing the top edge of her phone to her forehead, her other arm across her knees. She didn't know why she was crying, but the tears had started as soon as she disconnected the call. Her emotions were completely haywire at the moment. She thought she'd gotten a handle on her feelings for Lea - just a crush, she'd had crushes before, the threesome had been like releasing a valve.

But then Tori came along. Beautiful, sexy, strong Victoria Branigan. And Tori wanted her. And they got along well.

She wiped the heel of her hand across her eyes. While she'd touched herself, while the sounds of Tori and Lea making love had filled her head, she closed her eyes and remembered standing in the darkness under the L tracks. The way the shadows had fallen across Tori's face as she leaned in, the softness of her lips right before the kiss became harder, more intense. She brushed her hand over one cheek and remembered how Tori's palms had felt when she cupped her face.

The same hands, the same fingers, that had been inside Lea twenty minutes later. She shivered at the thought and dropped her phone into her lap, moving her hands to the back of her neck. She laced her fingers together under her hair and pressed back against them, tilting her head back to look at the ceiling.

She knew why she was crying. Because there was no way for this to end in anything but disaster. They might have a few more amazing nights together, she'd probably sleep with them together or separately a couple of times, but then the inevitable would happen. They would eventually fall prey to jealousy. To hurt feelings, possessiveness. She was crying because she knew how wonderful the next few weeks were going to be, and how crushingly painful everything after that would be.

The smart thing would be to pick up the phone, call back, and tell them it would be best to end things now. When it would hurt less, when they could chalk it up to a couple of good nights and get on with their lives.

But then she thought about Lea, idly running her fingers through her hair, twirling the ends around before letting the loose ponytail fall.

And then she thought about Tori, eyes shaded by her new baseball cap, covering her mouth when she laughed at something Janice had said or done.

She thought about how Tori's lips felt on hers.

She thought about her tongue on Lea's stomach, and Lea's fingers in her hair.

"You're going to let yourself get hurt," she said out loud.

"You're going to let yourself get absolutely devastated, you idiot."

Janice pushed her pants the rest of the way down, took them off, and stood up to take them into the bedroom.

She was just going to have to brace herself for the pain. Maybe that would make it more bearable.

Until then, she was going to enjoy the ride.

CHAPTER THIRTEEN

CHIEF MALLORY put *The Martian* on the big screen in the lounge after dinner, and Tori took the recliner in the back corner where she could hopefully go unnoticed. She took out her phone, opened an incognito window, and looked up to make sure no one was paying attention to her before she started typing. She tried 'open marriage' first, but the first results revealed that wasn't what she was looking for. She and Tori weren't going to seek out other people, they were only interested in one person. Google theorized she might be thinking of polyamory.

Before she could examine those results, Captain Gambol came in with a fresh bowl of popcorn. He glanced toward her as he settled into one of the armchairs right in front of the TV.

"Hey, Branigan. How did the wife like the game?"

She minimized the browser as if worried he could see the screen reflected in her eyes. "Oh, I didn't take Lea."

He gave her a look of disbelief. "You asked for two tickets. Who'd you take?"

Later that night, she would lie in bed and come up with a list of possible responses. But at the moment she felt as if there was a five-second clock running that would buzz if she didn't give an answer.

"A friend."

"You have a friend who isn't currently in this room?" Conrad said, not looking away from the screen. "I call bullshit."

"I have a lot of friends," Tori said. "Not all of us are social pariahs who only hang out with our spouses. It... it was a, it was this woman Lea and I know. Janice."

Annie looked up, putting pieces together in her brain but saying nothing.

Gambol was eyeing her suspiciously. "What's going on, Tori?"

"Drop it, Dave," Chief Mallory said.

Gambol shook his head. "No, no... something's up, Chief. What's so hard about saying you went to the game with your friend?"

"Nothing," Tori agreed. "I went to the game with our friend. Janice."

Freddy, the probationary officer who had remained silent to this point, said, "Wasn't Janice the name of that lady who asked you out?"

Mallory and Gambol both looked at him. Gambol said, "What are you talking about?"

Freddy looked at Tori. There was fear in his eyes. "Uh. I-I don't know. I just overheard something. I might have been making stuff up. I-I dunno."

"Someone asked you out?" Gambol was staring hard at her now, any humor drained from his voice. "And you took her to the game using my tickets?"

Tori realized where his anger was coming from. Gambol's marriage had shattered because his wife had an affair. Infidelity was something he could not abide.

"Dave," she said, pointedly not using his title. "Janice is our friend. Mine and Lea's both. I swear to you. Lea knew about the game. Hell, she helped me get ready for it."

Annie cleared her throat. "She's telling the truth, Cap. We talked about it. The lady didn't know Tori was married when she asked her out. When she found out about Lea, she backed off. They're just friends now."

Gambol seemed appeased by the defense. "If I find out you're cheating on Lea–"

"Whatever you're about to say," Tori said, "I accept the threat as already made. I'll never have to worry about it."

"Good."

The chief finally looked away from the TV, eyeing Tori and

then Gambol. "If you two are finished hissing at each other, how about we all relax and watch this guy grow potatoes on Mars?"

"Sounds good to me, Chief," Tori said.

Gambol nodded and settled back in his seat.

Tori relaxed and looked at Annie, nodding her gratitude for stepping in. She knew Gambol wouldn't do anything terrible. He might shun her around the station, but he would still have her back on calls. The worst he might do is transfer so they didn't have to work together anymore. She definitely didn't want that. He was a good man and a great captain.

She also didn't think whatever she and Lea were exploring was any of his business. He had his triggers, and she respected that. But she wasn't going to share private information just to make him feel better.

It did make her worry about what would happen if and when Janice became a much bigger part of their lives. There were probably going to be more dates. Sometimes Lea would be the one going out with her, sometimes Tori would be, and there were good odds they might run into David out in the world. What if all three of them were out at dinner? What if Janice and Lea were holding hands on top of the table? God, how many people would they have to 'explain~

"Are you okay?" Annie asked quietly.

Tori blinked her eyes, snapping herself out of the spiral. She hadn't even noticed Annie moving to sit next to her. Still, she nodded.

"Yeah, I'm fine. Thanks."

"Let me know if you need to talk later. Everything's cool with you and Lea, right?"

"Yeah. Everything is... amazing. Yeah."

Annie looked relieved. "Okay."

They watched the movie for a while longer before Tori's phone pinged. She glanced at the screen, saw Lea's picture, and swept her thumb across the screen.

Hey... busy?

She held the phone and typed a message with her free hand. *Matt Damon's life is in danger, but I think Jessica Chastain can handle it.*

There was a long pause, surprisingly long to Tori's thinking, and then a response arrived. *Chastain can handle anything.* There were three dots, and a second message popped up. *So I have a question...*

Lea was in bed reading a Whitney Otto book when her phone chimed. She put it down on her chest and smiled at Janice's name. It was a request for a video call, and she accepted even though she had already scrubbed her face and put her hair up. Janice's face filled her screen and Lea saw that she was also in bed. Her hair was down, and there seemed to be layers more of it than Lea remembered. She also had on a pair of black-rimmed eyeglasses that Lea found very becoming.

"Good evening, Miss Kozak. How are you?"

"I'm fine. I wanted to see how you were doing. Tori's working tonight, right?"

"Aw, you're sweet. I'm doing okay. No sirens tonight, at least not any I've heard. I was just reading before I went to sleep." She held up the book. "It's about being an artist and a woman."

Janice said, "Two things you know a lot about."

Lea laughed and put the book on the table. "Yes, I know a little bit. Did you have a good day at the restaurant?"

"It was good. It was great. We've been really busy lately. A *lot* of people are paying attention to the artwork. I've seen people taking pictures. The whole atmosphere of the place has changed. I really do think it was the piece it had been missing. It feels different now. Finished. I feel like I can finally relax there now, and it's great."

"Well, you're very welcome. Tori and I will have to come and see the place."

Janice said, "Yes! Yes, any time. I'll make sure you both got the royal treatment."

Lea slid down on the mattress until the pillow was under her head. "Oh yeah? You would treat us like queens?"

"You don't deserve anything less."

"Hmm. Hey, I've never seen your bedroom. Show me."

Janice looked past the phone. "Oh. Uh, okay, hold on..."

She put the phone down, the screen flashing a few colors and shapes before it settled on the ceiling. Lea saw a flash of thigh and black underwear under her night shirt as Janice scooted past the phone's camera. There were muffled sounds, the squeal of a drawer closing, and then the hollow thud of a door. Then Janice was back, flashing her thigh at the camera again as she climbed back into bed.

"Sorry," she said. "Dirty clothes and stuff. Ready?"

"Mm-hmm," Lea said.

Janice turned the phone and slowly panned across the room. Lea brought the phone closer to her face so she wouldn't miss any details. Hamper, bookshelf stuffed with hardbacks and paperbacks, coats hung on the back of the bedroom door, framed photos. She caught a glimpse of the black-and-white checkered pattern of Janice's bedspread.

"Wait, wait. Show me the blanket."

The camera tilted down. Janice smoothed it out with her free hand, straightening the material next to the mounds made by her legs.

"Like it? It's super soft and comfortable. And warm, warm, warm."

"It looks so cozy."

Janice turned the phone back to face her. "Maybe you'll have to try it out sometime."

Lea grinned and raised an eyebrow. "Well, I would, but I'm already in my pajamas."

Janice lifted her chin. "You saw my bedroom. Can I ask to see your pajamas?"

"Are you asking what I'm wearing?" Lea asked coyly, lifting the phone and pulling down the blankets. She was wearing a pajama set Tori had gotten her for Christmas one year. Dark blue with white lines on the collar and cuffs. She wasn't wearing anything under it, but the shirt was long enough to reach mid-thigh, so she figured she was safe from unintentionally flashing anything.

"You do look pretty cozy," Janice admitted. "Another night, then."

"Mm-hmm," Lea said, pulling the blanket back up. "That's a promise. Your bedroom is lovely, by the way."

Janice shrugged. "I'm pretty partial to yours. Good memories there."

Lea giggled and tucked her hair behind her ear.

Janice laughed. "I love that. Your giggle. It's cute. Women don't giggle anymore. Men ruined it too much."

"Well, I don't give a shit what men think," Lea said. "A laugh can be its own language, you know? Big belly laugh, little chuckle, polite laugh. A giggle is... it's..."

"More intimate?"

Lea nodded. "Exactly." She pressed her back into the pillow. "I like being intimate with you."

Janice chuckled. "Yeah. It's... good."

"I wasn't just talking about..." She cut her eyes toward the empty bed next to her. "The night we spent together just sleeping. You holding me. I thought I would only have that feeling with Tori again, but you made me feel safe and protected."

"You're more than welcome."

Lea pressed one foot on top of the other under the blanket. "I wish you were here now."

"I don't know if that would be safe," Janice said playfully. "Since neither of us are wearing pants. Far too much temptation."

"Sometimes it's good to give in to temptation."

Janice's smile wavered. "Yeah. B-but I agree with Tori. The next time anything happens~"

"She should be here," Lea said, nodding her agreement. Absolutely."

There was silence for a moment.

Janice cleared her throat. "But I wish I was there, too. For the record."

Lea worked her bottom lip with her teeth, then made a decision. "Hold on, please."

She went to her text messages and sent one to Tori. "Hey... busy?"

Janice smiled, chuckling. "What are you doing?"

"Sh. I just want to... hold on, she's answering.

A reply popped up. *Matt Damon's life is in danger, but I think Jessica Chastain can handle it.*

"Apparently she's watching a movie." She tapped her fingers on the back of her phone. She looked at Janice, holding eye contact. "I'm going to ask her if you and I can have phone sex. If that's okay with you."

Janice pulled her head back from the phone. A hair fell across her face, and she absently swept it away. Lea noticed her fingers were shaking. When she finally answered, her cheeks had flushed pink.

"Uh-huh. Yeah."

"Yeah?" Lea said.

Janice met her gaze again. "Yeah, yes. Ask her."

Lea nodded and typed her reply. *Chastain can handle anything.* Her fingers were shaking, too. *So I have a question...*

Shoot.

Janice and I are chatting. Video call. We're both in bed. She thought about what she might type next. Everything she could think of sounded too blunt or crass.

"What are you saying?" Janice asked.

"I can't figure out how to ask."

Janice cleared her throat. "Tell her that I want to be with you."

Lea laughed softly. "I can't say that."

"Then let me." She brought her other hand up and started typing.

Chiwetel Ejiofor and Mackenzie Davis were reading text messages from Mars when Tori's phone finally buzzed again. She had it open to Lea's messages, but the new one had come from Janice. She frowned and clicked on the name to open it.

I want to have phone sex with your wife.

Her face was suddenly very hot. She glanced at Gambol, then at Annie.

It wasn't how the conversation started. I just called to check in on her. We both want this to happen, but neither of us will go forward unless we have your blessing.

Tori glanced at the TV. She didn't know how much longer the movie had, but it seemed like Damon was a long way from getting home. She looked at Annie, who turned and raised an eyebrow. Tori motioned for her to stay put. Annie raised her other eyebrow, and Tori put a finger to her lips. Annie kept her expression neutral but it was obvious she was fighting a smile.

"I think I'm going to get a little shut-eye," Tori said, pushing herself up from the chair.

Gambol twisted to look. "I hope you're not leaving 'cause of me. I got carried away..."

"No, you're fine." She waved him off. "I've been around long enough, I'm used to you being a douchebag by now."

Gambol snorted and turned back to the screen. Tori wished everyone a goodnight, then headed up to her bunk. She considered putting a sock on the doorknob, but she knew that any signal she sent to Annie would also be deciphered by the guys. Annie walking in on her was less embarrassing than the guys figuring out what she was up to, so she decided to risk it.

She closed the door, took off her shoes, and climbed under the blankets. She opened her texts again and started a group with both Lea and Janice.

On one condition, she sent.

She reached under the blanket and unbuckled her belt. She

unbuttoned her pants, and pushed them down just enough for her to do what needed to be done. When she was ready, she sent her follow-up message.

"She wants a picture," Lea read.

"From both of us." Janice looked up from her screen. "Do you think she means now, or... is she asking for nude pics?"

Lea said, "Were you planning to take off your clothes for... for what we're about to do?"

"I was just going to touch myself," Janice said. "And talk."

Lea nodded. "Me too. So pictures of how we look now. We'll take the pictures and send them, then go back to the call, okay?"

Janice said, "Yeah."

Lea closed the app and sat up. "*Vaya*," she muttered as she opened her camera. She held the phone out with her arm twisted, trying to find the best pose. She knew Tori liked her breasts, but she also liked her legs. There was no good way to get both into the shot, though she tried a few angles. Nothing she saw looked sexy. It was all just awkward and strange. She finally held the phone out in front of her with both hands and snapped a selfie.

Tori might like her breasts and legs, but she *loved* her eyes. She sent that, then settled back down and opened the video call app again. Janice was waiting, lying on her side with the phone positioned so it looked like Lea was next to her in the bed. Lea rolled onto her side and did the same with her phone.

"Did you send it?"

"I did," Janice confirmed.

A new text appeared and, judging by the movement of Janice's eyes, she had also received it.

Tori: *I'm in bed, too. Go ahead. I'm going to be thinking about what you two are doing.*

"She's going to be masturbating," Lea said.

"Yeah... I saw."

Janice wet her lips and looked into the screen as she lifted her shoulder and pushed her hand under the blankets. Lea's breath caught in her throat when Janice gave a quiet gasp.

"Are you wet already, Janice?"

"Yeah," Janice said.

"Good. I saw your underwear when you got out of bed earlier." She moved her free hand down her chest, across her stomach. "Black. So sexy."

"What color is your underwear?"

"I'm not wearing any," Lea admitted. "When I showed you earlier, I thought you might get a peek. But I didn't care. I wanted you to see."

Janice sighed and closed her eyes. "You should have shown me."

Lea lifted one leg just long enough to slip her hand between her thighs, then trapped it there. "I'm wet, too."

"Good," Janice said, almost like she was dreaming. Her eyes were open, though, staring hard at Lea. "You're so beautiful."

"Thank you." Lea's fingers curled on the back of her phone, lightly scratching the case. "You're gorgeous. Tori is looking at your picture right now. She's touching herself thinking about you."

Janice moaned. "God..."

"I wish I could see her. See her pleasure herself... watch her come for you."

"I'd watch you watch her."

Lea giggled.

"God, that giggle... fuck..."

"I'm sorry," Lea said.

"Don't be sorry." She shifted and leaned closer to the camera. Her eyes were closed now, but her lips were parted. "Call me that name..."

Lea purred, "Rico." She rolled the R and saw Janice shudder. "Rico, Rico..."

"You can never call me that in public," Janice said.

Lea laughed softly and pressed her face into the pillow. She forced her eyes open and stared at the screen. Everything about Janice was so light. Blue eyes, blonde hair, pale skin... Tori was darker everywhere. Tanned, brown eyes, brown hair. They were complete opposites of each other and yet...

"You're so pretty," Lea said.

"You're gorgeous," Janice replied, closing her eyes and breathing in deeply, then releasing it with a sigh. "Oh, fuck. Keep talking. I liked it when you were talking..."

"What do you want me to say?"

"Anything, anything," Janice said.

Lea moved the phone closer. She was using two fingers on herself in a slow rhythm. "Janice," she said. "I think of watching you with Tori, and I can't control myself. You were so beautiful together. It was the sexiest thing I've ever seen, and I can't wait until we're together again. I want to watch you take her clothes off. I want to hear her moan when you put your fingers inside her..."

Janice whispered Lea's name and then opened her eyes. "I'm close, Lea."

"Me too," Lea said, moving her fingers faster. "Look at me. I'm right here with you, *querida*." She watched Janice's bottom lip shake, and the way the skin around her eyes tightened as she struggled to keep them open, and she knew she was on the edge. "Now, baby, now," Lea purred. "I'm going to finish with you. Make yourself come for me."

Janice moaned and arched her back. The phone slipped out of her hand, briefly aimed at the ceiling before she recovered it. Lea squeezed her eyes shut and pressed her face into the pillow to muffle the moan that slipped out of her mouth. Goosebumps erupted on her neck and marched up her spine, making it feel like her hair was standing on end. She shuddered and shook, then exhaled slowly and turned her head back to the phone.

"You're beautiful when you come, Lea."

She chuckled sleepily. "You are, too. Next time I'll whisper even dirtier things in your ear."

"While Tori is doing other things?"

"Mm-hmm." Lea chuckled. "We are very good at teamwork."

Janice laughed. "I've seen it first hand. Can't wait." She pushed her hair out of her face. "I-I admit, I have no idea what we do now."

"Now we say goodnight, and I call Tori to help her finish."

"I wish I could eavesdrop on that."

Lea said, "We'll tell you all about it."

"God, you two..." She put her hand over her eyes, shook her head, and then waved. "Goodnight, Lea. Thank you."

Lea blew her a kiss. "Goodnight, Rico."

She disconnected the call, rolled onto her back, and dialed Tori's number.

Tori had one hand between her legs, the other holding her phone facedown on her chest. She was breathing slowly, eyes closed, keeping herself right on the edge as she thought about her wife and their new whatever-she-was a few blocks away. She opened her eyes and lifted the phone, turning on the screen again to reveal the picture Janice had sent. She was sitting up with her back against the headboard, her free arm wrapped around a pillow. Her head was tilted down and she was looking through her eyelashes with a come-hither look, her lips curled into a sly grin.

"Fuck," she moaned, putting the phone down again. She lifted her hips to meet her fingers and curled her toes.

Her phone rang. She moved her thumb to dismiss the call until she saw it was from Lea. She answered and put it to her ear.

"I'm close," she said without preamble.

"Come for me, *querida*," Lea said, her voice rough with post-orgasm tiredness.

Tori breathed hard. "Did... d-did you..."

"We came together. I said dirty things to her, and I watched her make herself come for me. Now I want to make you come, my love."

"Lea..."

"Victoria. I want to be there with you. I want to taste you. I want to kiss you when you finish."

Tori grunted through grit teeth, well aware of the group downstairs. "Lea..."

"Your hand is mine," Lea said. "I'm going to make you come right now, Victoria. Come on, baby. Come for me."

She did as she was told, squirming against her mattress, lifting her hips and pushing her pillow up toward the headboard with her shoulders. She wanted to cry out, wanted to let Lea know exactly how this felt, but she restrained herself to a long and guttural moan before she fell back onto the mattress. She draped her arm across her face as she caught her breath, listening to Lea on the other end of the phone.

"It's better when we're all together," she finally said.

Lea giggled. "Yes. But this will do in a pinch. *Te amo.*"

"*Te amo.*" She kissed the air next to the phone. "I'm going to let you go to sleep, beautiful lady."

"Okay. Goodnight, my love."

"Good night, *querida.*"

They hung up and Tori pulled her clothes back into place. She went to the bathroom, splashed some water on her hot cheeks, then raked her fingers through her hair to make sure it wasn't too mussed from the writhing she'd just done. Once she felt presentable, she went back downstairs in her socks.

The whole lower level was dark, making the building feel eerie. She could hear the sounds of an outer space rescue echoing from the lounge. She went into the kitchen, turned on the light over the stove, and searched for a snack she could make before trying to get some sleep. She'd gathered the fixins for a sandwich when Annie joined her.

"I assume that was Lea?" she said under her breath. "Good things or bad things?"

Tori raised an eyebrow and smiled.

"Oh-ho, okay. Good for you. I was prepared to 'accidentally' fall asleep on the couch if you needed a little space."

Tori chuckled. "I appreciate the thought." She leaned to one side and looked toward the lounge. All she could see from the kitchen was the blue light of the TV flickering on the dark walls. "Did the guys say anything?"

"Freddy asked if you were okay. I think Gambol was just glad you were busting his chops again, and Chief was just happy you two didn't need to be separated."

"Busting his chops? How old are you?"

"I'll be eighty-six in June." She pointed at the sandwich. "Make me one."

"Make your own, grandma." She pushed the bread across the counter.

Annie started putting her sandwich together, letting the silence linger before she finally gave in. "So... what exactly *is* going on with~"

"I don't know." Tori lowered her voice further. "But I think it's going to be... a thing."

"And you and Lea are both okay with that?"

"I think so," Tori said. "She's eager, and I'm enjoying it all so far. I don't know if I would've felt comfortable with doing this if it was anyone but Janice. But yeah, Lea and I have talked it through enough times that I'm not worried about if it's the right step. I just..." She sighed and rested her hands on the counter. "You saw what happened in there. If it does end up becoming a 'thing,' then I either have to sit the guys down and talk about a very intimate part of my life~"

"Which is none of their business."

"Exactly. Or I'll..." She sighed wearily. "I'll have to essentially go back in the closet. Lying to my coworkers about who I'm spending time with and why. I don't want to do that again. I *hated* that."

Annie nodded. "Look, you don't have to make a decision now. Now you're just figuring stuff out, right? So until the three of you know everything, you shouldn't bring anyone else in."

"Thanks, Annie. And thanks for being a sounding board."
"If you were really grateful you would've made me a sandwich."
Tori threw a napkin at her.

Chapter Fourteen

Tori came into the apartment quietly, putting her things on the couch instead of the floor. She took off her shoes and walked down the hall in her socks. She paused at the bedroom door and, when she didn't hear anything within, slipped inside. Lea was stretched out on her side of the bed with an arm across her stomach and the other tucked under the pillow. Tori went to her side of the bed, took off her pants and shirt, and got into bed under the blankets.

Lea stirred, murmured, and lifted her head to look over her shoulder as Tori pressed against her from behind.

"Oh hello," she said sleepily.

"Morning." Tori put her hands on Lea's stomach and kissed her neck. "How'd you sleep?"

Lea squirmed and stroked Tori's arms. "Wonderfully. So many good dreams."

"Good." Tori slid one hand down lower and pressed her palm against the front of Lea's underwear. She skimmed her lips over Lea's neck. "Last night was hot."

"Yes it was... But this morning could be even better, mm?" She put her hand on top of Tori's, then used her other hand to move her underwear. She guided Tori's fingers inside. "Mm, yes. Much better when it's someone else's hand."

Tori licked the shell of Lea's ear, then nipped the lobe. Her hand explored and her other hand slid over the curve of Lea's breast.

Then she stopped.

Lea whimpered. "Don't tease me, *querida...*"

"I'm not." Tori lifted her head and pulled her hand away, resting it on Lea's stomach.

Lea sensed the tension in the room had shifted and rolled onto her back to look up at her wife. Tori's mind was working around a strange block of feelings, chipping away at it until she could put it into words. Lea reached up and stroked her cheek, then tucked a strand of hair behind her ear.

"Victoria?" Lea asked, worry creeping into her voice. "What's wrong, baby?"

"I don't know." She looked at Lea. "I'm... I-I don't know."

"Are you tired?"

Tori shook her head. "No. I just feel like... last night... you and Janice. You thought of me, you asked me for permission before you did anything. If we're... if this is going to turn into something else, I think we need to show her the same consideration."

Lea said, "You want to ask her permission to make love to your wife?"

"Yeah. Kind of." Tori winced. "That's weird, isn't it."

"No," Lea said, stroking Tori's cheek again. This time she let her fingers hesitate on the jawline. "I think, um... I think we need to look at this as something new, yeah? If we're going to explore it at all, we shouldn't think of it as you and me, plus her. We need to start things as equal as possible. We obviously have far more history together, we are married, we live together. We can't change that. But we can treat her like an equal in the physical part of our... of the relationship."

Tori sat up and reached down for her pants. She retrieved her phone and sat cross-legged on her side of the bed as she dialed.

"This is going to be a weird conversation," she said as the phone rang. "How do I even phrase--"

"H'llo? Tori...?"

"Janice. Hi. Sorry. Did I wake you up?"

"Yeah, I don't care, it's okay. Are you okay?"

Tori said, "Yeah, it's fine. I'm home with Lea. Something came up. And we needed to talk to you about it before anything else happened."

Janice sounded more awake now. "Okay. If last night went too far~"

"No," Tori said. "Last night was amazing. But it does involve what happened." She looked down at Lea. "I wanted to wake Lea up with sex. We started fooling around, and then I realized that last night, you asked before you did anything. I wanted you to know how much I appreciated that."

She held out her free hand. Lea took it, laced their fingers together.

"And I wanted to show you that we're all on the same footing," Tori said. "So I didn't want to do anything with Lea unless I knew it was okay with you."

Janice was quiet for a long time. "You're her wife."

"I am. And for the past three years, that's been all we needed to know. But if we're going to turn what we have into something different, then the old rules don't apply. Right? If we bring you into this, I don't want you to feel... to feel like you're..."

"Extra," Lea suggested.

"Extra," Tori said. "We want you to feel, a-and know, that you're a full partner in this. Lea and I aren't the arbiters of what happens in the bedroom. We all get a say."

Janice was quiet again. "Wow."

"You don't have to answer right away. If you want to~"

"You can have sex with her," Janice said. "Whenever you want. You don't need my permission. I appreciate you giving me the power to say no. But that's not something I want. I don't want to dictate your lovemaking."

Tori said, "Are you sure?"

"I'm positive. Just give her a kiss from me, huh...?"

Tori smiled. "I will. And Janice... the same goes for the two of you. If I'm at work and you're here... or you want to do another video call..."

"Are *you* sure?"

"Yes." Tori looked down at Lea, who nodded. "And the same goes for you and me, apparently. I think it makes sense, right? We're... the three of us... we're creating something here. And it shouldn't be dictated by when we're all available or in the mood or in the same room."

Janice said, "As long as you're sure."

"We can revisit the rules if things get uncomfortable," Tori said. "But I think for now this is the best course of action."

"I agree. And... since I have you on the phone, we're still on for dinner tonight? And then..."

"Absolutely," Tori said. "Text what time we should show up and we'll be there."

"I can't wait. Have fun."

Tori hung up and looked at Lea, who raised her eyebrows. "Well...?"

Tori grinned and pounced on her wife.

Lea was setting up for a photoshoot when the light in the studio suddenly changed. That was a major downside of having one wall be mostly glass; she could easily fall victim to the smallest change in the weather. She looked over her shoulder and discovered the darkening wasn't due to clouds but because of a man hanging on the other side of the glass. She sucked in a breath of air and pressed a hand against her chest, quietly swearing before she realized he was a window washer and couldn't see in.

"You nearly gave me a heart attack," she said.

He was seated on some sort of platform, so small that she could barely confirm it was there. His torso was wrapped in a bright yellow harness that looked secure, but she couldn't imagine trusting it enough to focus on work. A bucket was hanging from one side, and he was casually sweeping his plunger across the pane. Lea walked over and stood in front of him. She crossed her arms over her chest and watched him work.

"I know I'm being selfish," she said to him suddenly. "I know that! You don't think I know that? I absolutely adore Tori. And by some miracle she feels the same for me. She might even love me more, which makes me feel warm and safe." She folded her hands against her chest. "People go their entire lives without that. You know? I found it. I have it, and I cherish it, and now I want more? I want someone else, just because she makes me feel... safe and protected and..."

She dropped her hands and started to pace.

The window washer moved lower.

"And it's not just me. I know that. I'm not that egotistical. None of this would have happened if Janice wasn't attracted to Tori. I saw them together." She laughed and shook her head. "There is... there is definitely something there. And I liked it! Oh!" She mimed her mind being blown. "I loved watching my wife fuck someone else. Isn't that crazy?"

The window washer swept away a sheet of suds.

Lea sighed. "They were beautiful together. I watched Tori... and it's different to, to watch and see someone you love like that from the outside." She interlocked her fingers and pulled like she was trying to stretch. "I thought there would be jealousy. 'Get off of my wife!' you know? But... it was Janice. And I was so..." She moved her hands. "I wanted to see it, I wanted it to happen. To keep going. I didn't even care if they did anything to me as long as I could keep watching them."

She licked her lips and faced the window washer again.

He swept away another block of suds.

"I barely know Janice. But I barely knew Tori when I knew I wanted to spend the rest of my life with her. And... she was... when she was so reluctant to get married, I made my peace with the idea we might never have that traditional thing. And I was content with that. Tradition is overrated, right? We need to do whatever is right for us, now. Too many people have been miserable because of what they thought tradition was supposed to be."

He nodded.

Lea blinked at him and stepped forward. "Hello?"

"Sounds like you know what you want," he said. "I say go for it. See what happens."

Lea jumped back a step. His voice was hollow and flat, but she definitely heard what he had to say. She swore under her breath and turned her back on the window, hurrying out of the studio. She didn't stop until she reached the reception desk. Kathleen looked up, startled by her sudden appearance.

"Mrs. Contreras? Is everything okay?"

"The windows in my studio are one-way, right? The outside is mirrored. People can't see into the studio from the outside."

Kathleen looked back down the hall, confused. "Um. No?"

Lea's eyes widened. "Yes, they are."

"No, if the sun is shining on them, like it does in the morning when we first come in, they're mirrored. But that only lasts for about an hour. The rest of the time, they're just windows."

She felt her cheeks redden. "Oh no."

"Is everything okay? Do you need me to call someone?" She reached for the phone.

"No! No. Um, it's... it's... f-fine. I just... never mind. Thank you, Kathleen."

"You're welcome, Mrs. Contreras..."

Lea went back down the hall, dreading her arrival in the studio. She had left the door open and peeked around the door frame. The window washer was gone. She breathed out in relief and went in, closed the door and went back to the photoshoot she'd been preparing before she was distracted.

"Go for it," she muttered under her breath. "See what happens."

She sighed and shook her head.

"Next time I'm going to rant in Spanish."

CHAPTER FIFTEEN

WHEN THEY arrived at Canvas, the hostess escorted them to the same table they'd had the first time. To Tori, it felt like months had passed since that night. Her entire relationship with Lea had changed in ways she never would have suspected. She squeezed Lea's hand as they sat across from each other. Lea looked down at the place settings, then scanned the room.

"What's wrong?" Tori asked.

"Hm? No. Nothing. I'm just wondering how..." She gestured down at the table. "It's... there's a, um, priority? I guess? Like if we sat on the same side and Janice sat across from us, it would make her the odd one out. But sitting like this, she has to sit next to one of us, and that puts someone else on..." She trailed off when she saw how Tori was looking at her. "I'm overthinking this, aren't I?"

Tori smiled. "I think so. It's just seating. There are going to be a lot of situations like this. If we go somewhere on the train, two of us can sit together and the third will have to be in another row. And if we go see a movie, who sits in the middle? There's no right answer. So we'll just play it by ear. Right now, sitting across from each other makes sense."

"Okay." Lea sighed, then breathed in deeply. "Okay. Okay."

"That was three okays. Give me one more, make it even."

Lea grinned and reached her hand across the table. "Okay."

Tori took it. "There's going to be a lot of stuff like this. We can't make a checklist and decide ahead of time what we want to do. We'll just figure it out in the moment, okay?"

"Okay." She realized she'd said the same word again and hissed at herself.

Tori laughed and brought Lea's hand up. She kissed the knuckles. "I love you."

"*Te amo*," Lea said.

Janice came out of the kitchen a minute later. She was dressed in a dark blue blouse and black slacks, her hair up. It might have been the lighting, but Tori thought her skin was sparkling as she crossed the dining room to their table. She bent down to kiss Lea on the cheek, lips grazing the corner of Lea's mouth. Lea turned her head slightly and gave Janice a second, more direct kiss. Janice smiled, straightened, and bent down to kiss Tori on the lips as well.

"Hi," Janice said, settling into the chair next to Tori's.

"Hello," Lea said.

"Hi," Tori said.

Janice cleared her throat and looked around the room. She caught the eye of a waitress and motioned her over.

"This is Rebecca. She's great."

"We'll be sure to tip well," Tori said.

Janice said, "Oh, you're not paying."

Tori shook her head. "A wise man once said even if the food is free, the service isn't."

Janice nodded. "Sounds like my kind of guy."

Rebecca arrived and took their order, promising to return briefly with their drinks. Once she was gone, Janice cleared her throat.

"So who wants to begin? I'm not sure..."

"I'll start," Lea said, looking at Tori for confirmation. Tori nodded, and Lea continued. "We talked when Tori got home from work. After we're done here, Tori is going to go home with you. She has a bag ready to go, it's outside in my truck. She'll drive you home and I'll take the train back. You two can spend the night together. And tomorrow night, while Tori is at work, you'll come spend the night with me."

Janice sat up straighter. "Oh." She looked at Tori. "Are you sure about that?"

"We discussed it," Tori said. "We want this to be an evolution of our marriage, which means~" Rebecca came back with their drinks, and Tori stopped until she was gone. "Which means treating you like an equal. It means being together, not just the three of us but... all of us. Individually and together."

"No, I understand that. The logic of it. But you two have been together a long time. I don't want something that seems like a good idea on paper to blow up in our faces once things have happened."

"I read about this thing." Lea's phone had been facedown on the table, and she picked it up and swiped the screen. "It's called, um, compersion. It's basically the opposite of jealousy in a relationship. It means that when I see Janice with you, I'm happy that she's bringing you pleasure. Whether it's in the bedroom or going to a baseball game with you. I get pleasure from the pleasure she gives you. I know it doesn't take anything away from what you get from me, or what you give to me in return."

Tori nodded. "That's how I feel knowing Janice is there if you need someone when I'm at work."

Janice took a deep breath and let it out. "Okay. I'm obviously on board with it, I'm... y-you're both amazing. But I keep thinking about the fact we really are still just getting to know each other. And this is moving so fast. I'm worried it's just... it's just the idea of, um, being with someone new. That new relationship endorphin rush tricking us into thinking it's a good idea."

Lea shrugged. "Maybe. But we're not doing anything that can't be undone. We're testing the waters."

"We both wanted to sleep with you," Tori said. "And when we did, there wasn't a feeling that the itch had been scratched. We wanted more."

"We still want more."

Tori said, "And if you get uncomfortable about anything, or feel like we need to tap the brakes, just say the word."

"Absolutely. You can decide you don't want Tori to come home with you~"

"No!" Janice looked bashful at her outburst, then looked at Tori. "I obviously want her to come home with me. I'm just a little concerned about how much I want it."

Tori smiled. "Welcome to the club."

Their food arrived shortly after. Janice waited until Rebecca had gone before she waved her fork over the plate.

"One of these days we'll have to arrange to have dinner *after* the... physical activity..."

Lea and Tori laughed. Lea said, "It's hard when I use food as a love language and you literally own a restaurant. But we'll figure it out."

"Yeah." Tori picked up her glass. "Here's to figuring it out as we go along."

Lea and Janice tapped their glasses against hers.

I'm going home with someone's wife, Janice thought.

They were sitting next to each other on the train, and Tori had a backpack between her feet. They hadn't said much after saying goodbye to Lea outside the restaurant - a long hug with Tori and a kiss for Janice, followed by a sly "Have fun" before Lea got into her truck. Janice didn't know if the silence was awkward or not. Maybe Tori wasn't much of a talker on the train. Maybe she was preparing herself for a night in someone else's apartment, in someone else's bed, while her wife was home alone. As the train slowed for an upcoming station, she decided to just go for it.

"Are you okay?" she asked.

Tori looked at her and nodded. "I'm fine. You?"

"Yeah. I was just..." She waved her hand vaguely between them. "I wasn't sure if we should be talking or not. I don't really talk on trains. And it's not like I had things to say and I was holding back. I just was... I wanted... W-we've established that this whole thing is built around communication. Doubts, fears, concerns..."

"Do you have~"

"No," Janice said quickly. "The only doubts I have are about my apartment, and if it's ready for... guests. Oh. Oh god..."

Tori grinned. "If it helps, I'll hang out in the hallway while you make your bed."

Janice chuckled. "Thank you. I appreciate that. I think it's presentable. I-I like to keep the place tidy. But I didn't expect..."

"I don't judge people based on apartment tidiness. Especially if they're busy building a business from the ground up. That doesn't leave much time for dusting."

"No," Janice said.

She reached out and put her hand on Tori's, intending for it to just be a quick pat. But her hand decided to linger. Tori looked down at it, then looked at Janice before she turned her wrist and linked their fingers together. Janice looked into Tori's eyes and slowly shook her head.

"This is so strange. When we met, I thought it would be wonderful to date you. Then I met Lea, and I kind of threw out all those fantasies and mental images of where the date would go. Now the door is not only open again, this is all actually happening. I feel like if I woke up and this was all a dream, I wouldn't be surprised."

"Do you have a lot of dreams like this?"

"Well..." She looked around the train. A coffee cup was rolling loose near the doors, and a woman hunched in the corner was dressed in at least five layers on a night that barely required a hoodie. "They're not *exactly* like this."

Tori laughed and leaned in. Her lips brushed against Janice's. Janice accepted the gentle kiss, and returned it with a stronger one, parting her lips as an invitation. Tori accepted it, and squeezed Janice's hand. When they pulled back, Tori furrowed her brow.

"Why are you minty?"

Janice smiled bashfully. "Before we left the restaurant, when I went into the office to grab my things? I have a little emergency kit in the desk drawer. I took a second to brush my teeth."

Tori grinned. "Well, I appreciate the effort. The kiss was... *very* nice." She looked around to see if anyone had taken notice. "I haven't kissed anyone else since I met Lea. And before her, there was a dry spell of a few years. Focusing on the career, and before that being in the closet. So it's been maybe a decade since I kissed anyone who didn't taste like Lea."

"Wow," Janice said. "I'm honored."

Tori squeezed her hand.

"Harrison is next," a voice said from a speaker overhead. "Doors open on the left at Harrison."

"That's us," Janice said.

They stood and left the train. They were on the street before Janice realized they were still holding hands. She thought about letting go, but she wasn't holding on very tightly. Tori could have pulled her hand away if she wanted to. So she left it and brushed her thumb across the back of Tori's fingers as she led her down the street to her building.

When they arrived, Tori stepped back and waited for Janice to unlock the door. "If you need some time to straighten things up, I can run into the bathroom and get ready."

"That would be great." Janice pushed open the door. "Bathroom is to your left, at the end of the hall. Second door."

Tori made a show of covering her eyes as she stepped in, looking around her fingers to make sure she didn't bump into anything as she fled. Janice watched her go and then did a quick recon for anything embarrassing she might have left out. She grabbed a few empty glasses and a bottle of beer, crossing into the kitchen with two loping strides to hide them in the sink. The bedroom was right off the living room, and she opened the door to peek inside.

"Bed made, good girl," she whispered to herself. She kicked a pair of socks under the duvet.

She went to the sound system. She scrolled through her playlists and chose something unobtrusive but mood-setting, then found a good volume. She looked toward the closed bathroom door, ran her hands through her hair, and started pacing as she waited for Tori to return.

Tori shrugged out of her shirt. She pulled it back up onto her shoulders, adjusted the collar. She fixed her hair. She started to button her shirt, stopped. She had unbuttoned it while she brushed her teeth, so she wouldn't accidentally get anything on it, but now she couldn't decide if she should keep it on. Her underwear wasn't particularly sexy. Why hadn't she put on something sexier? Probably because she didn't really *own* sexy lingerie. Lea preferred her in briefs, boxers, panties, tank tops... comfort was key, and Tori couldn't argue with that. But now, how was she supposed to strike a seductive pose in an outfit with far too many Hanes logos sewn into it?

She had to decide soon, or else Janice might think she had cold feet. "Fuck it," she said, and kept the shirt on but unbuttoned. She had already taken off her shoes and socks. A time saver for later. Another time saver would be taking off her pants, so she did that. She stepped out of them, leaving them as a pool on the mat. She left her underwear on, though. Going outside bottomless would come off a little too... she didn't know what, but she didn't want to be it.

"Okay. Now or never."

Tori checked her teeth to make sure they were clean, exhaled, sighed, and went back out into the living room.

A song was playing loud enough that she thought she recognized it, but soft enough that she couldn't quite identify it. Janice was sitting on the edge of an armchair and jumped to her feet, smiling nervously as she waited for Tori to cross the room.

"Your apartment is lovely."

"Thank you."

"Thank god there aren't any dirty dishes anywhere. That would be a dealbreaker."

Janice's eyes widened, then relaxed. "You peeked."

"Maybe a little." Tori stepped closer.

It was the wrong apartment, it was the wrong beautiful woman, it was everything wrong, but it was right at the same time. She wanted to be here. Lea wanted her to be here. There were no lies, no deception, nothing but open and honest want and desire. Janice watched her carefully, and it was obvious she was letting Tori steer the ship tonight.

She put her hands on Janice's hips, then leaned in and kissed her before her brain could twist her up in knots. Janice leaned into her, arched her back, and Tori moved her hands to Janice's ass. She cupped it through her pants, squeezed, and Janice made a noise of approval. When she pulled back from the kiss, she caught Tori's bottom lip with her teeth and held it for a moment before she let go.

"Where's the bedroom?" Tori asked.

Janice backed up, pulling Tori with her. There must have been a speaker in the bedroom, because the volume of the music didn't change as they passed into the darker room. Janice ran her hands over Tori's biceps, squeezed, and sighed before she angled her head for another kiss. Tori flexed as subtly as she could and felt Janice's fingers tighten.

At the bed, Janice sat down on the edge of the mattress. Tori started to kneel in front of her, but Janice whispered, "Wait, wait." She twisted, grabbed one of the pillows, and dropped it on the floor.

"Such a gentleman," Tori said as she knelt on it.

"You have no idea," Janice said, cupping Tori's head and pulling her in for a kiss.

Tori rested her hands on Janice's thighs, slowly moving them higher as the kiss continued, deepened, became more passionate.

When she reached the button, Janice muttered, "mm-hmm," without breaking the kiss. Janice felt a chill, thinking of how often Lea responded to questions with that same closed-mouth affirmation. Her head swam, and suddenly it felt like Lea was there, watching them, and it made her heart beat faster. Her hands shook as she unfastened Janice's pants and tugged them down. She leaned back and Janice lifted up, moving just as much as necessary to get the pants out of the way.

"I feel like this is the first time," Janice said breathlessly.

"Yeah," Tori agreed. "First time without Lea." She looked up into Janice's eyes. "Are you okay?"

Janice breathed a laugh. "Okay is not the word for what I am. If I was hooked up to a heart monitor, it would probably be freaking out and telling me to call a doctor. But given the circumstances..." She kissed Tori's lips. "I'm as okay as I could hope for. You?"

Tori nodded. "Very okay."

"Okay."

Janice leaned back. Tori kissed her way down Janice's chest, undoing the buttons on her blouse and pushing it open to kiss along the cups of her bra. When she saw goosebumps, she ran her tongue across them and felt Janice shiver under her. She spent a few seconds on Janice's belly, her bottom lip brushed over the barely-visible blonde hairs there. She skimmed the back of her hand over Janice's thigh and felt the muscles tense.

"Tori..."

"Call me Victoria when I'm this close to your pussy."

Janice hissed through her teeth and put one hand in Tori's hair. "Victoria, please."

Tori kissed her through her underwear, and Janice lifted her hips to meet her tongue. They both gasped. Tori massaged Janice's inner thigh with one hand while the other pushed the cotton panties aside. She wet her lips and flicked the tip of her tongue against Janice's folds, teasing her before moving up to kiss her clit. She moved her hand up and teased with one knuckle, then two, and eased one finger inside.

Janice moaned, writhed, and pulled Tori's hair. "Sorry..."

"Don't be. You can be a little rough..." She put her tongue back to work, holding Janice down through the shudder that followed.

"Victoria, don't stop."

Tori opened her eyes and looked up, watching Janice's face as she came. She waited until the twitching stopped, until Janice stopped making strange quiet sounds somewhere between whimpers and moans, and then slid up her body. Janice's eyes were closed but she reached for Tori without looking, pulling her close, kissing her. She moved a hand between them. Tori straddled Janice's waist and guided her hand between her legs.

"Here," she whispered against Janice's mouth, moving the cotton aside for her.

"You're so wet..."

"Yes."

Janice opened her eyes and looked up at Tori. "Hi."

"Hello. Make me come, Janice."

Janice's eyes widened, narrowed, and then she moved her hand faster. Tori kept her eyes open as she moved against Janice's fingers. She was close, breathing heavy, lips parted, she could feel the sweat beading on her forehead, and then...

"Come for me, Victoria."

She closed her eyes and gave into her orgasm. Her entire body went rigid, her shoulders hunched. When she relaxed, she dropped down onto Janice and shuddered. Janice wrapped her free arm around her, the other trapped between their bodies. Tori shivered again when Janice started peppering kisses across her forehead.

"Are you okay?"

"Ask me again after the second time," Tori said.

"The second... oh. Okay." She chuckled. "Just let me know when you're ready."

Tori smiled and closed her eyes. She just needed to catch her breath. She was sure it wouldn't take too long.

CHAPTER SIXTEEN

AFTER TORI fell asleep on top of her, Janice remained still and listened to music until her playlist ended. She stroked Tori's hair, her arm, anything she could reach with her unpinned hand. When the last song played the apartment became quiet. Janice considered repositioning herself, waking Tori up just enough so they could get into a more comfortable position.

But honestly, she was already pretty comfortable. It had been a long time since she'd had a lover fall asleep on top of her. She liked hearing Tori breathing, the weight of her. She liked smelling their sweat. So she just stayed where she was. She closed her eyes and waited to see if she could fall asleep as well. She would have liked to finish getting undressed, but she had slept under worse conditions.

Tori woke up after close to half an hour, right after she started making quiet snoring noises. She lifted her head slightly and muttered, "Lea...?"

"Just me," Janice said quietly. She brushed the hair away from Tori's face. "You okay?"

"Yeah." She blinked up at Janice. "I fell asleep."

Janice smiled. "You were working pretty hard."

The corners of Tori's mouth twitched. "Do what you love..."

"C'mon, get up," Janice chuckled. "My mattress is much more comfortable than my body."

"I find that hard to believe, but okay."

She put her hands on either side of her shoulders, and Janice was treated to the far-too-brief sight of Victoria Branigan doing a push-up directly on top of her. It was almost enough to inspire her to ask for another round, but she could see the exhaustion in Tori's eyes. They would have plenty of time in the morning.

She got up to turn off the light while Tori turned herself so her head was on the pillow. Janice took off the rest of her clothes, feeling ridiculously awkward as she stretched out on top of the blankets. Tori put a hand on her hip to pull her closer.

"How do you feel?" Janice asked.

"Good. Weird. But I think that's to be expected, right? But it's a good weird. Not a sad or panicked weird." She smiled. "I can't wait to tell Lea all about this. And I can't wait to hear how tomorrow goes with you two."

"Maybe you can help me decide what to wear. A special outfit."

Tori raised an eyebrow. "Oh, that might be fun. You don't need to do much to get Lea excited, just show up and be yourself. But I have some inside information that might throw some gas on the fire."

"I can't wait." She leaned in and kissed Tori. "Goodnight."

"Night."

She planned to watch Tori fall asleep. She was positive there was no way she could sleep tonight, not with the energy currently buzzing through her blood. But at some point she must have fallen asleep, because she was aware of Tori getting out of bed and seeing her silhouette move through the darkness to the bathroom. Then suddenly Tori was sleeping next to her again, spooning her.

"Victoria," she whispered, trying it out.

"I'm here," Tori said. "Go to sleep."

Janice put her hand on top of Tori's and followed her directive.

Janice felt like a clown. She knocked on the door to Lea and Tori's apartment and stepped back, looking down at herself. Tori had sworn to her that this outfit would go over well, and Janice had no reason to distrust her. But she had barely spent any time going through the closet before she pulled out a dry-cleaning bag, peeked inside, and declared it the winner. She'd held it out to Janice like a trophy.

"This. You're wearing this."

"*That?*" Janice said. "No, come on. I have so many sexy outfits..." She sorted through the options. "Well, okay, maybe not *sexy*. But seductive. Or... or... accentuating my breasts. Look, you wouldn't believe how this makes my tits look."

"Your tits don't need the help," Tori said, and Janice had laughed despite herself as the dress was taken from her and put back in the closet. "It's this."

Tori had never been stiff or awkward around her, but this morning was the first time she seemed to be totally at ease. She was smiling easier, laughing. Her walls were down. Janice knew she was seeing a side of her that very few people, maybe only Lea, got to see, and that was enough to make her feel like she'd accomplished something. And if trusting her recommendation was the cost of that accomplishment, she was willing to risk looking like a clown.

The door opened and Lea swept out to greet her. "You're here! I... I..." She took a step back, her smile fading as she ran her eyes down Janice's body.

I knew it, she thought. *This was a prank.* She didn't even know why she'd kept the old waitressing uniform. Black slacks, white shirt, black necktie, and a black vest. It made her look like a butler. At work she'd always had to wear her hair tied back, but this morning it was down and wavy. She hoped that made her look casual, but now all her doubts came rushing back.

"Tori told me to wear this," she said.

"I owe her a present, then," Lea said under her breath. "Rico..."

She moved closer and slid her fingers up Janice's tie, pinching the knot. She pulled her and gave her a passionate, probing kiss that almost knocked Janice off her feet. To save herself from falling, she wrapped her arms around Lea and half-carried her back into the apartment. She kicked the door shut behind them, turned, pressed Lea against the wall, and returned the kiss with redoubled passion.

"I love a woman in a suit," Lea said between kisses. "Tori... mm, Tori doesn't like how she looks in them." She flicked her tongue across Janice's mouth. "I disagree. But I never make her wear them." She stepped back and made a sound that could've been called a growl. She ran her hands down the front of Janice's chest and then moved back up to her hair. "*Dios mio...*"

"What time do you have to be at work?" Janice gasped.

"Took the day off."

Janice smiled and walked Lea toward the bedroom. "Good."

When they reached the bed, Lea sat down on the mattress and started working on Janice's belt. "Unbutton the shirt, but leave it on," she said.

"Tie?"

"Loosened."

Janice dropped the vest and unbuttoned her shirt as Lea pushed her pants down. She put her hands on Janice's ass and leaned forward. Janice put her hands on the back of Lea's head and closed her eyes, rising onto her toes to offer a better angle for what Lea was doing with her tongue.

She didn't know how she'd gotten to this point. She'd never been the type of person to jump out of bed with one person and into bed with another. Even breakups required weeks of recovery before she was ready to be with anyone else. And the fact the two women in this case were married... She felt like all their conversations shouldn't matter. Something inside of her, some vestigial indoctrination, should scream that this felt too much like an affair, that it was wrong, that they should stop...

"Don't stop," she whispered.

Lea squeezed her ass and curled her tongue. Janice shivered and gripped Lea's hair tighter. She looked down and saw Lea looking up at her, and she managed to arrange her quaking lips into a smile. Lea smiled as well, winked at her, and then used her tongue and bottom lip to perform what Janice could only call a finishing move.

Afterward, she pushed Lea down and laid on top of her. They kissed, and she tasted herself on Lea's lips as Lea slipped her hands into the open front of Janice's shirt.

"That's how you respond to a woman in a suit?" Janice asked once she'd caught her breath.

Lea giggled and kissed Janice's cheek. "Good?"

"Yeah, no, I'm just wondering why Tori hasn't quit the fire department and become a maître d'. Or a magician. Or... hell, a professional suit-wearer."

Lea laughed. It was a throatier sound than her giggles, coming from a deeper place, and it made Janice shiver in places that had just calmed down. She pressed her lips to Lea's in an attempt to capture the sound. Lea brushed her fingers down Janice's cheek and Janice broke the kiss to turn her head and capture the thumb in her mouth. She bit it, then sucked it into her mouth. Lea cooed and kissed her ear.

"I didn't intend to attack you like that," she said. "You ambushed me. I had a whole thing planned. I was going to make you lunch."

"Oh." She kissed Lea's palm. "I could go for a little snack."

"Yeah? What are you hungry for?"

Janice smiled and slipped down Lea's body, kneeling next to the bed and reached under Lea's dress to take off her panties.

Lea dropped her arms out to her sides, palms up. "No-o-o... you're going to kill me..."

"It's okay," Janice said, resting Lea's legs onto her shoulders. "If you need help, I know an emergency professional we can call..."

Lea smiled, bit her lip, and surrendered.

"I spent all last night thinking about what was happening at your apartment," Lea said.

"I hope you didn't drive yourself too crazy."

Lea shook her head. "No, but any details you want to share..." She made a go-ahead motion and then winked.

They were sitting at the dinner table, Lea in her underwear and Janice wearing her pants and unbuttoned dress shirt. Janice hadn't wanted Lea going to any trouble for lunch, so they'd agreed to make sandwiches and share a bag of potato chips. It reminded Janice of awkward high school lunches with girls she had crushes on, but this time the feelings were requited. She found Lea's bare foot under the table and trapped it between hers.

"Maybe we should wait until Tori is here and we can act some things out for you."

Lea's eyebrows shot up and she smiled. "Ooh, yes. I like that idea. Let's do that for sure. I can wait until tomorrow."

Janice's smile faded. "Tomorrow. Right." She shook her head. "That has to be hard getting used to. Just having her gone so often."

"I don't think I am used to it," Lea said. "The panic attacks and everything. I don't mind being alone, but the worry is always there. I miss her. I get lonely sometimes. It's hard feeling like you only have a part-time partner. But she has the same problem. She spends half her time at the station, sleeping in a twin bed. It was probably much harder in the days before cell phones and video calls and all that. I'm glad technology took off just in time to make my marriage a little more bearable."

Janice chuckled and got up to get a drink. "I'm glad I'll be able to help with the loneliness. For you, at least. It doesn't seem particularly fair to Tori, does it? You get double the attention, but she has to share time during her days off."

"I know," Lea said thoughtfully. "I talked to her about it, and she doesn't think she'll feel left out. She is usually pretty good at... you know... at analyzing herself like that. So I'm taking her word for it unless I see evidence otherwise. We'll just have to make sure she gets extra-special attention to make up for it."

Janice looked over her shoulder with what she hoped was a sultry expression. "Hm. Luckily we have a whole day to come up with things we can do when she gets here."

Lea smiled. "You're a little evil, Rico."

"Oh, just wait until I'm *really* comfortable with you two."

Lea bit her lip and leaned forward, intrigued.

Tori opened the apartment door and slipped inside, scanning the living room for clues about what had happened in her absence. The dinner table was spotless, nothing had been left out on the coffee table. Janice's shoes were next to the door, which so far was the only evidence she was in the apartment. Tori crouched down to untie her shoes and stepped out of them before she continued her search. The bedroom door was open and she stopped on the threshold to peek inside.

Janice was facing the door, holding a fast-asleep Lea in her arms. Tori felt an unexpected surge of emotion at the sight so strong that she nearly backed up into the hallway to compose herself.

She might have done it if Janice wasn't awake. She looked up when Tori appeared in the doorway, blinked sleepily, and lifted the unpinned hand to wave at her.

Tori waved back. Then she pointed at Lea and mimed lifting her.

Janice laughed silently and shook her head. She waved Tori over.

Tori unfastened her belt and pushed her pants down, pulled her shirt over her head, and climbed into bed behind Lea. She spoon against her, reaching over her to put her hand on Janice's hip.

"Morning," Tori whispered.

Janice looked to see if Lea was still asleep.

"Don't worry about her," Tori said softly. "As long as we're not obnoxiously loud, she'll sleep through anything."

"Anything?" Janice said, then pressed a kiss to Lea's forehead.

Tori grinned. "Almost anything." She kissed Lea's temple and slid her hand around to Janice's ass. "But I'm open to a little test."

Janice kissed Lea's eyebrow. Tori shifted positions and brushed the hair off Lea's shoulder. She bent down and kissed her neck. Janice kissed Lea's eyelids and then bent down to kiss her lips. Janice's hands brushed against Tori's stomach as she pulled Lea closer. Tori kept kissing, licking, and sucking on Lea's neck as she looked up and watched Janice press a series of small, quick kisses to Lea's lips.

After the third, Lea pressed her lips together. On the fourth she started responding, wetting her lips with a sweep of her tongue before Janice started kissing her properly. Lea moaned, then opened her eyes and looked down.

"Wait, what's... oh hi..."

Tori smiled. "Hi."

Lea laughed once and then kissed Janice again, moaning into her mouth. Tori moved her hand from Janice and slipped it between her and Lea. She discovered Lea wasn't wearing underwear and growled, moved her mouth up to Lea's ear. She nibbled gently and stroked her thighs, then back up to nestle her hand between them. A moment later she felt a hand on top of hers. She looked up and met Janice's gaze, nodded her agreement, and let Janice guide her fingers.

Lea squirmed between them. "I can't handle this," she whimpered, pressing back against Tori before she thrust forward against Janice.

"Then tell us to stop," Janice said.

"No, Rico, don't, never," Lea gasped. She kissed Janice, turned her head and kissed Tori in the same breath. She ran her hand down Janice's arm, reached back to squeeze Tori's hip, pulling her closer. She twisted so that she could look up at them.

"Kiss," Lea said. "Kiss over me, please..."

Janice and Tori didn't hesitate to comply. Tori pressed against Lea's back and felt Janice's leg slip between Lea's as their lips met. Lea sat up and kissed Tori's cheek, then Janice's, then whispered something in Spanish that Tori couldn't hear. Tori broke the kiss with Janice and pressed her lips to Lea's cheek as Janice kissed her lips.

Tori sat up and leaned across Lea to kiss Janice's ear. She pulled her hand out from under Janice's.

"Make her come," Tori whispered to Janice. She slid her hand down Janice's back, over her ass, and pressed her fingers between Janice's legs. "Make our girl come."

She felt a shiver run through both the women in her bed and realized there'd been a shift in her mind. At some point during the past forty-eight hours, it started feeling wrong to think of Lea as 'my wife.' She didn't know if Lea felt the same about her. It was a conversation they all needed to have later, together. But for now she pulled back, her body still pressed against them, watching Janice, watching Lea.

Janice gripped Tori's fingers as Lea arched her back, one hand grabbing Janice's shoulder and digging in so hard that it must have hurt. Tori bent down and kissed Lea's fingers, then slid her lips to Janice's skin.

Janice made Lea come, and moments later Tori made Janice come, and for the next few minutes, they leaned against and on top of each other to catch their breath. She moved her hand from between Janice's legs and rested her fingers on Lea's lips. Lea closed her eyes and slowly, gently sucked them while looking into Tori's eyes.

It wasn't how they'd planned to end their two-day experiment, but Tori couldn't have thought of a better way to start down their new path.

CHAPTER SEVENTEEN

"WE SHOULD probably work out some ground rules." Tori, in a plain white undershirt and briefs, using the tips of her fingers to turn a cup of coffee in small increments.

"I don't like the word 'rules'." Lea, in a fire department T-shirt and nothing else, hair mussed, feet up on her chair so she could hug her knees. "Marriages don't have rules, relationships don't have rules and, and guidelines, right?"

"Actually they do." Janice, with her back to the wall in an unbuttoned dress shirt and panties, her hair up in a sloppy attempt to keep it out of her face. "They're usually unspoken things, like... like, um, chore responsibilities and stuff like that. Who is responsible for taking out the trash, who does the dishes, does a grocery run..."

They had relocated to the kitchen table after they were able to extricate themselves from the tangled sheets and blankets. Lea had gone to take a quick shower while Tori and Janice made breakfast. Janice was surprised at how well they worked together, moving around the relatively cramped kitchen without colliding or stepping on each other's toes. A hand on the shoulder to guide Tori out of her way, or a whispered, "'Scuse me..." if she was blocking a drawer Tori needed was enough to keep things moving smoothly.

That was what Janice was thinking about when Tori mentioned

rules, and it was why she agreed with Lea.

"I think writing down an actual do/don't list is a bad idea. We probably don't know half the speed bumps we're about to deal with. If we make a list now, today, we might be tempted to try and fit every situation into the existing boxes. And doing it on a case-by-case basis will force us to have conversations instead of just drawing a line between allowed and restricted."

Tori thought about that. "Okay, I see your point. But there are some things that are definitely allowed, right? The three of us can sleep together in any, um... configuration. We don't need to give each other permission. We already talked about that and decided it, right?"

"Right." Lea reached out and took Janice's hand. "From here out, we're thinking of this as 'the three of us,' not two people plus another."

Janice nodded. "I appreciate that. And we're not seeing anyone else. This isn't an open-door~"

Lea said, "Absolutely not," at the same time Tori said, "No," and they smiled at each other. Lea continued. "This isn't an open relationship. This only happened because it's you."

Janice looked down, hoping it would hide the redness in her cheeks. The idea that these two amazing women had opened their home, their marriage, to her... Still, she wanted to slam the doors behind her just to make sure no one else tried to sneak in.

"Something else we need to establish early," Tori said. "How much are we telling people?"

"Right." Janice looked up. "Well, I've talked things over with my kitchen manager, Evan. He knows what's going on, pretty much, but he's a vault. He's like a therapist to me."

Tori said, "Annie knows. She's a member of my company."

Lea smirked. "I would call her Tori's work wife, but I don't want to make things any more complicated than they already are."

Tori chuckled. "What about you, Lea? Who have you been talking to about this?"

"Oh. Um. No one."

Janice and Tori both looked at her. "What do you mean 'no one'?" Tori asked.

"Well, there was a window-washer," Lea said. "But I don't think he counts because I don't know how much he actually heard."

"Lea, we've talked about this." Tori kept her voice measured. "It doesn't have to be a therapist, but you need someone to talk to.

Someone who isn't involved in–"

"I'm not going to tell my receptionist about who I'm sleeping with," Lea said. "And I don't have any assistants long-term, you know that. They're students, they're temps, they come and go all the time. I can't form a relationship with them strong enough to trust them." She pushed her hair out of her face. "It's fine. I don't need a confidant."

Janice said, "We all need someone to talk to. Even if it's just to sort out our thoughts. I probably would have gone crazy pacing back and forth in my apartment if it wasn't for Evan."

"Fine, I'll talk to one of you."

Tori shook her head. "You can't talk *to* us *about* us. You need an impartial third party."

"Well, I think it helps if the person is biased toward her," Janice countered. "Evan is biased toward me, Annie is biased toward you... The mark of a good confidant is someone who only wants the best for you. That's why it can't be me or Tori. If you came to me, it would put Tori on the outside."

Lea made a face. "Fine. I'll try to find someone to talk to. Even if it is a therapist."

"Good," Tori said.

"I think that's a good move," Janice agreed. "It will prevent a lot of grief in the long run."

Tori held her hands out to indicate the table between them. "Look at that. I guess Janice was right about communicating. Much better than rules."

Janice smiled. "We have to look at this as something that's constantly evolving. Even if..." She stopped herself, preparing for what she was about to say. "We moved *very* fast into this. I'm not saying that's a bad thing. I was pressing down on the accelerator as hard as either of you. But we have to at least consider the possibility this is all just confusing 'new and exciting' with something more. You two have been together for a long time. You miss the thrill of first dates, getting to know a new person. We might all just be swept up in the hormones of what's happening."

"I suppose that's possible," Lea said, looking at Tori.

"The problem is that we won't know for sure until it has a chance to simmer. Once we get used to each other, we'll know if it's something real. And if time passes and you realize this isn't something you want to pursue in the long-term..."

Tori held up her hands again. "No, we don't have to talk about this."

"No, we really do," Janice argued. "Because you need to know that I want you to be absolutely honest with me. Even if it's painful. The alternative is clinging to something after it stops working. And that wouldn't just ruin this, it might ruin the two of you."

Lea shook her head. "I don't see that happening. But..." She spoke slowly. "You have my word. We will always be transparent about our feelings. Even the bad ones."

"Even the bad ones," Tori agreed. "So what do we do now?"

Lea stood up and pulled her shirt down so it draped her thighs. "Now," she said, gathering the plates, "I am going to clean up the wonderful breakfast my ladies made for me. And the two of you are going to go take a shower together."

Tori and Janice looked at each other.

Janice shrugged. "The lady makes a strong argument."

Lea grinned over her shoulder as she took the dishes into the kitchen. "Have fun."

Tori and Janice were already halfway to the bathroom, shedding clothes as they went.

Once the water was warm enough for them to get in the shower, Janice stood with her back to the faucet. Tori reached past her to catch the spray in cupped hands, which she used to douse Janice's hair. Janice tilted her head back and smiled as Tori began working out the tangles.

"So we're not going to fool around?" Janice asked.

"I wouldn't say no," Tori said, "but I've also been called to enough slip-and-falls to know that shower sex usually isn't worth the effort."

Janice laughed and looked down, moving her foot to tap one of the seashell decals affixed to the bottom of the tub. "I guess that explains these."

"Yep. I've gotta do what I can to keep my girls safe. So no shower sex. But shower kissing..." She bent down and brushed her lips across Janice's. "Shower touching..." Janice rested her hands on Tori's hips and leaned into the kiss, the water spraying onto her shoulders and splashing up to sprinkle against Tori's jaw and cheek. "Shower caressing..." She moved her hands up Janice's back, skimming the soft skin on either side of her spine.

She thought about what Janice had said a few minutes ago, about whether their feelings were just excitement of being with someone new. She'd considered that possibility after their first night together. It had been on her mind since they started seriously talking about exploring something new and long-term. She'd lusted for people before, even after she and Lea were married. It was nothing she had ever acted on, obviously, but she'd had feelings, urges. There were crushes.

This was something else. Kissing Janice, knowing Lea was in the other room, her nerves still buzzing from waking them up... This was something she'd never felt before. This was definitely something new. As scary as it was, she felt an equal measure of excitement for what lay ahead.

She broke the kiss and looked down into Janice's eyes, marking the smile on her lips and the way her eyebrows arched as she waited for Tori to do or say something. She searched for the right words, but nothing presented itself. Finally she just kissed Janice between the eyebrows and pulled her closer.

"I think we all got very lucky," she whispered into Janice's hair.

Janice put her arms around Tori and rested her head against her chest.

"I'm supposed to talk to someone," Lea said, eyes on the road. "Someone who is on my side, who has my best interest at heart, even if it means brutal honesty and truth."

"Okay." Kathleen's voice was cautious. "You know I'm not a therapist, right? Or a priest or..."

"No, no, I know," Lea said. "I've done the therapy thing, and I don't think it's worth the cost for what I got out of it. I know it saves people's lives. I know it's vital and important. I'm not badmouthing the profession." She sighed and shrugged. "I just don't think there's a, um... I don't... The things I want to discuss don't require a therapeutic response. Does that make sense?"

"Let's say it does so we can move on."

Lea sighed, nodded, flexed her fingers on the steering wheel. "Thank you."

They were driving to a photoshoot in Lea's truck. She'd realized while they were loading her gear into the backseat that she wouldn't have trusted very many people with her equipment. Surely that had to mean something. She glanced over at Kathleen, and then back out at the road.

"It's about sex. So it might be inappropriate. I don't want you to be uncomfortable. So if I cross a line, just let me know and I'll, we can just pretend this never happened."

Kathleen chuckled. "For the record, it's better to have a conversation like that in a place where I'm not... you know, trapped."

"Shit! Right. It's not like you can just ask me to let you out." They were driving on Lake Shore Drive, the city to the right and the lake stretching out to their left. "I'm sorry. Never mind."

"No, it's fine. I'll let you know if I get uncomfortable. So what's going on? Problems with your wife? It's Victoria, right?"

Lea nodded. "Yeah. I mean no! No, not problems with her, not at all. I just meant, yes, her name is Victoria. Tori." She blew out air and shook her head. "Ay *ay ay*... okay. Tori and I are exploring a new... a new aspect to our relationship. It started with a threesome. We met a woman we both found attractive and interesting, and we agreed to invite her to join us." She flinched and looked at Kathleen. "If you want me to stop at any time..."

Kathleen shook her head, still chuckling. "It's fine. I'm a big girl. Please, go on."

"Okay. If you're sure. So it went well. It went really well. And it turns out we, um, we... we wanted more."

"Four?"

"No! For goodness sakes!"

Kathleen laughed and held her hands out. "Well, it was the natural progression."

Lea's cheeks burned. "You are very much troublesome. Gee. No, we wanted more with Janice. The-the woman we... that it happened with. We didn't want it to be just a thing we were doing with her for fun."

"Oh!" Kathleen stopped laughing. "You guys are polyamorous?"

"No. I don't know." She narrowed her eyes. "Maybe. I think Tori looked up something. We both still love each other very much. But this thing with Janice? It's something more than just fun. And it's more than just sex. We both spent time alone with her. We enjoy her company very much. Tori and I both admitted that if we'd met her when we were single, we would have been interested in her romantically."

Kathleen was nodding. "That sounds very cool. And you're all having conversations, right? Being mature and honest about your feelings?"

"Mm-hmm," Lea nodded. "We've agreed that if any one of us

feels uncomfortable or like a line is being crossed, we'll talk about it."

"That seems smart and healthy." Kathleen looked out the window. "So, um, sorry, but why are you telling *me* all of this? Unless you're just bragging to a single woman that you've got *two* partners, which seems a little more cruel than I thought you were."

"Oh no. No! No." She shrugged and flipped one hand up. "I don't know why I'm telling you this. They told me I had to tell someone! They both talk to people at work about it, so they said I needed to do it, too. It was either you or a therapist. And I trust you."

Kathleen lifted her chin. "Aw, really? That means a lot."

She was silent again for a few minutes, long enough for Lea to get off Lake Shore and start navigating toward their destination. She finally started talking again as Lea parked in front of the building.

"I think this is just laying the groundwork for future conversations. Like... things are fine with the situation *now*. But eventually there will be something you need to get off your chest or vent about. People need that in every relationship. I imagine it's twice as important in a polyamorous one. Things are going to come up for sure." She looked at Lea again. "And you want to talk to *me* about it?"

Lea said, "I don't know. I'd like to. I'd be willing to. I trust you with my work stuff, and that level of trust... I can't really explain it. But my career depends on this equipment. If something happened to it, there's no guarantee I'd be able to replace it. So it's my lifeblood. And I let you load the truck. So I figure that has to mean something. But if you're uncomfortable~"

"Not at all," Kathleen interrupted. "I'd be honored."

"Really?"

"Yeah. You think I take a whole day off to help the lawyer down the hall type up depositions? You're my favorite tenant. I'd love to be a sounding board for you."

Lea nodded emphatically. "Okay then, it's settled. You are my doctor-priest. But I'm only paying you to be my assistant."

"That seems fair."

They got out of the truck and began unloading. "Oh," Lea said, "if you ever want to talk to *me* about a relationship, it absolutely goes both ways."

Kathleen chuckled. "Yeah, I'll keep that in mind in the unlikely event I meet someone. But hey, if you and your wife find any other strays, feel free to send them my way. You're starting to look greedy."

Lea laughed and swatted at Kathleen's arm. "Go, get inside. You're on the clock."

She watched Kathleen go and shut the truck, hoisting her bag up onto her shoulder to follow her inside. Maybe having someone to talk to wouldn't be the worst thing in the world.

CHAPTER EIGHTEEN

THERE WAS less sex than Tori expected over the next few weeks. They did have sex, obviously. She and Lea slept together, and she knew Lea and Janice slept together when she was on duty. They'd spent a handful of nights in the same bed. But Janice still had her own apartment and slept there as often as she stayed at their apartment. Tori had brought up the idea of cohabitation, but Lea and Janice both thought it was far too early to make decisions about that. So some nights, when Tori was at the station, Lea packed a bag and slept at Janice's place.

But by and large, deciding where to sleep was just about scheduling. They talked about whether Tori would be home or not, and if Lea would pack a bag.

The majority of their time was spent with actual dates. Janice took Lea to the Field Museum. The three of them went out to dinner, branching out from Canvas to explore the city's other offerings. Tori really did find the seating arrangements awkward and stressful. What did it mean if Janice was in the middle? Was sitting her on the outside excluding her? Riding the train was a nightmare if they couldn't get a row of seats under the window.

"You're worrying about nothing," Lea gently chided her whenever Tori hesitated to choose a seat. "Just sit! We're not ranking anyone, we're just sitting down."

She was getting a little more comfortable with it. Sometimes Janice was to her right, sometimes she was in the middle. All she could do was try to make sure they alternated regularly. Putting Janice on the outside would only become a problem if it became her normal spot.

And while sex wasn't the focus of the time they spent together, it was... phenomenal. She couldn't believe how amazing it was. She was having sex with the woman she loved, with the addition of having sex with someone exciting and new. Getting to know Janice - what she liked, what got her off - was as thrilling as watching Janice explore her and Lea.

She found herself thinking about them at inopportune times. Never at a fire, of course. She'd been on the job too long to let herself be distracted by things like that. But after the fire was out, on the drive back to the station, she would wonder if Lea and Janice were awake, if Lea had woken up and Janice was comforting her.

This particular shift, it was mid-afternoon, so she could safely assume they were both at work. It was three weeks into their exploration, depending on when they marked the start of things. They were in the kitchen, gathered around the table in anticipation of the lunch Freddy had been promising since the night before. Tori had a pad of paper in front of her and was doodling what had started as a monster but was quickly evolving into a cityscape.

Conrad was sitting across from her with one foot up on the table. He had his phone out to show Annie texts from a woman he was seeing so she could analyze them for deeper meaning.

Chief Mallory came into the room from the hallway, pausing to slap at Conrad's foot as he passed. He snapped his fingers to get everyone's attention, changing direction long enough to wave Gambol in from the break room where he was watching a court show. Mallory started talking as soon as everyone was present.

"All right, just a heads up. They don't need us, but we've been alerted to a fire in progress in the Loop. Engine 32 already got pulled in, so we're on tap to cover their calls."

"Figures," Conrad said. "Big flashy fire in the Loop and we get stuck playing substitute."

Gambol said, "I'm sure the family whose house you save will be just as grateful as the mucky-mucks in Dayton Square."

Tori's head snapped up from her drawing. "Sorry, what?"

Mallory looked at her. "What's up?"

"Did you say Dayton Square?"

"Yeah, fourth, fifth, and sixth floors."

The room was suddenly unbearably cold to her. "That's Lea's building." Tori wasn't aware of pushing her chair away from the table, but she was suddenly standing up. "Lea's studio is in that building."

Conrad was already sitting up straighter. "What floor?"

"Eighth," Tori said, her voice small. "I think eight. I'm p-pretty sure. I haven't been in a wh-while." She had her phone in her hand without consciously taking it out of her pocket. She dialed and started to pace as she listened to the buzz. "Come on, Lea... answer the damn phone..."

There were so many reasons she might not be answering her phone. Hundreds. But suddenly she couldn't think of a single one that involved her being alive and unhurt.

"If she got evacuated," Annie suggested, "she might have left her phone behind."

"Or she has it, and it isn't charged," Freddy said from the stove.

Tori nodded to them, but she had barely heard what they said. The call went to voicemail. *Hi-i, hello. You've reached Lea Contreras...* She swore under her breath, disconnected, and dialed the studio's number.

Chief Mallory was also on his phone. "I'm going to see who's in charge down there, Branigan. We'll find out what's going on."

"Thanks, Chief." Another voicemail, this time the professional one. All their operators were busy, apparently. *"Fuck!"* She resisted the urge to throw her phone, but only barely. She dialed a third time, Lea's personal cell again.

Gambol turned to Mallory, his voice low. "How bad is the fire?"

Mallory shook his head without answering, which was enough of an answer for Tori. She lowered her phone and started to dial a fourth time, but then she realized she needed to make another call.

"I need to call Janice."

Annie sat up straighter. Freddy said, "Who is Janice?"

"Janice is..." Tori had her phone to her ear, listening to another buzz of a ringtone, her brain too frazzled to think about how to phrase her answer. "Janice is our partner."

"What?" Conrad said. "Partner in what?"

"Hey, Tori," Janice said in her ear.

Tori turned away from the others. "Janice." She could feel tears threatening as she walked out of the kitchen, bracing her hand against the wall. "There's a fire downtown. In Lea's building. It's below her floor. I don't know if... I don't know what it means. If it m-means anything. But she's not answering her phone." She realized the phone was trembling against her ear, which meant her hand was shaking. She squeezed her fingers tighter.

"Are you there?" Janice's voice sounded like it was coming from the other side of a tin-can phone. "A-are you, did you get called?"

"No."

"What can I do?"

Tori felt a tear roll down her cheek. "I don't know. Nothing. I just wanted to tell you. I thought you deserved to know. I should have waited until I knew more..."

"No, I'm glad you told me." Janice sighed, a watery sound that made fresh tears fill Tori's eyes. "Will you let me know if you~"

"Absolutely," Tori said in the middle of the question.

"~hear anything... Thank you."

Tori wiped at her eyes with the back of her hand. "I'll let you go. I don't... I-I'm here if you want to call back or text or whatever. Unless I'm on a call. Or..."

"I understand. Thank you for telling me, Tori."

"You're welcome. Talk to you when I know more."

She hung up, took a few steadying breaths, and walked back into the kitchen. As she expected, everyone was staring at her. Gambol seemed to be fuming, arms crossed and lips pressed together in a tight line.

"Hey. Janice is~"

"No one's business," Annie interrupted. "I told them it's none of their concern."

"Thank you, Annie." She looked at Gambol. "But I don't want any misconceptions about who Janice is or what she means to me. Or to Lea. She's our partner. She's not my mistress, she's not Lea's girlfriend. The three of us are together. We're in a relationship. There's openness and honesty on everyone's part. Nobody is cheating on anybody. There are no lies or deception. Just three people who care about each other very much. Anything beyond that is no one else's business."

Gambol finally met her gaze. She raised her eyebrows at him.

"Clear?" she asked.

He nodded tersely.

"Good."

Mallory cleared his throat. "I, uh, I talked to the guy in charge down there. Ben Hoffman. He says the fire is contained for now. They're still working on evacuating the upper floors."

Tori worked her jaw back and forth and nodded. "Thanks, Chief."

"No problem."

Tori sat down again and stared at her phone. She knew it was pointless to keep trying. But she had a vision of Lea's phone sitting on a table, ringing into an empty smoke-filled room. She imagined Lea retrieving it once everything was over and seeing only a paltry handful of missed calls. *Oh, you only called me four or five times...? I thought you loved me.* She knew it was ridiculous as she dialed again and put the phone back to her ear, now just waiting for the familiar voicemail message.

"Hi-i, hello. You've reached Lea Contreras..."

An hour passed without any substantial updates from Dayton Square. Tori didn't honestly expect to hear anything. The firefighters on the scene had enough on their plate without calling with a play-by-play. Tori spent most of her time in the apparatus bay lifting weights and hitting the heavy bag, sweating out her frustration and fear as best she could.

Annie came down and found her. "Hey. Anything I can do?"

"Help me steal the truck and drive it downtown?" Tori asked, out of breath. "Come on. It'll be fun. We can be rogue firefighters."

"I was thinking more along the lines of spotting you on the weight bench. But sure, let me see if I can find the keys."

Tori chuckled. "Thanks. And thank you for standing up for me earlier."

"It was just the truth. No one needs to know what happens in your bedroom."

"Gambol would've made it an issue sooner or later."

"Yeah, probably." Something at the front of the garage caught Annie's eye and she stood up straighter. Tori couldn't see what it was because the truck blocked her view of the open bay doors. Her voice changed to a 'dealing with the public' register. "Hi, can we help you?"

"Hi. Um, I hope so. I'm looking for Tori Branigan."

Tori recognized Janice's voice and stepped into sight. Janice looked gorgeous, jeans and blue sweater, her hair down. It looked like she had been crying, but she smiled with relief when she saw Tori.

"Hi," she said. "I know I probably shouldn't be here. But I couldn't think of anything else I could do, and I was going crazy at the restaurant, and I—"

"Hi," Tori said, ignoring everything else Janice was saying.

She cupped her face and kissed her. Janice laughed softly, or maybe it was a sob, and returned the kiss. When they parted, Tori rested her forehead against Janice's.

"Thank you for coming."

"Of course."

Tori inhaled and looked into Janice's eyes. "*Te amo.*"

Janice's eyes widened. "*Te amo,*" she said, and kissed Tori again.

Tori reached for Janice's hand, lacing their fingers together. Janice squeezed. The kiss ended, and Tori stepped back. She looked over her shoulder to see Annie standing half-turned, arms crossed, examining a spot on the floor.

"Annie Vest," Tori said, "this is Janice Kozak. Janice, Annie."

"Nice to meet you," Annie said. "I've heard a lot about you."

"Yeah, Tori's mentioned you, too." She sniffled and wiped at her eyes. "Sorry you're meeting such a sobby, emotional wreck version of me."

Annie grinned. "Hey, we all have that side." She moved toward the door. "I'll leave you two alone. I'll be hanging out in the lounge if you want some privacy."

"Thanks, Annie."

"No problem. Nice meeting you, Janice." She turned and disappeared up the stairs.

Once they were alone, Tori turned to Janice. "You can stay here if you want. If we get a call, I'll have to run out of here at ninety miles an hour, but—"

"I want to be here for you," Janice said, taking Tori's hand again.

Tori smiled. She brought Janice's hand up and kissed the knuckles. "I love you."

"I love you, too," Janice said.

They kept their hands tightly clasped as Tori led her out of the apparatus bay, up to her room, where they could lean on each other until they received news about the woman they loved.

CHAPTER NINETEEN

THE SMOKE was starting to become a problem. It should have dissipated quickly since they were outside, but it seemed to cling to her clothes. Lea put her fist to her mouth and coughed as discreetly as possible.

"Are you okay?" Kathleen asked.

"Mm-hmm." Lea opened her gear bag, took out a small case of Tic-Tacs, and popped one into her mouth. Sucking on candy sometimes helped. She glanced over her shoulder at the source of the smoke, an Amazonian woman in a skintight leather skirt and a leopard-skin blouse. She had been stalking around the location in stiletto heels like a ferocious bird, pausing to examine anything she found distasteful. And she seemed to find *everything* distasteful.

Luckily she wasn't the one in charge of the photoshoot. That was Paul Knox, the man with a salt-and-pepper beard that reached mid-chest. He was the manager for Journey Snow, the 'Aussie phenomenon' that had recently taken over the music world. Lea couldn't see much difference between her and the Biebers and boy bands of the past, but somehow she'd already become a superstar without ever releasing an album.

Lea had been hired to photograph the cover, as well as art for the liner notes and promotional material. Journey's security was so tight that Knox had refused to do the photoshoot anywhere other than a place they'd already vetted. They wanted to be absolutely sure no fans could get in to harass Journey. Lea didn't mind, she had no problem setting up wherever a client wanted. Today that location was the Honeycomb, a fiberglass pavilion in the Lincoln Park Zoo. At the right angle, the curve of the sculpture perfectly framed downtown Chicago with the Willis Tower front and center. She didn't know how an outdoor location in a public place could be more secure than her building, but again, she worked at the whims of the client.

Lea had known it would be a difficult shoot as soon as they arrived. Knox walked up to her with a black box, the lid open, and waited as if she should know what he wanted her to do. She saw five or six cell phones inside.

"Do I take one?" she asked.

"You leave one," he said. "Both of you. It's a Faraday box. It blocks any cellular signals and prevents you from shooting any video or taking illicit photographs of today's shoot."

Lea pointed at Kathleen, who was carrying a camera bag. "You do know why I'm here, yes?"

He shifted his weight from one foot to the other and seemed to inflate with irritation. "You are here to take authorized photographs. We will go over the photos you take here and choose which ones will be used for the finish product. Any candid or behind-the-scenes photos are forbidden. Keeping everyone's phones in this box makes that much easier to enforce. Your phones will be fine and they will be returned to you when the session is finished."

Lea sighed and took her phone out. She turned it off and put it in the box. Kathleen stepped forward and did the same. He nodded his thanks and closed the box, carrying it away from them. Both Lea and Kathleen watched to see where he put it, then looked at each other.

"I don't know what I hate more," Lea said. "The fact he took it, or how much I hate that he took it. That's a sign of addiction, right?"

"Well, it's not great," Kathleen said. "But on the bright side, I'm right there with you."

Lea tried to look at being disconnected from her phone as a good thing. She tried not to mess with the stupid thing when she was working anyway, so it didn't matter if it was in her pocket or in a box somewhere.

Journey Snow was a teenager with shockingly white hair and

skin so pale it had to be enhanced by powder. She also bleached her eyebrows to near-invisibility and drew large circles around her eyes with makeup. Lea didn't know what the intention was, but she thought it made the poor girl look like a cartoon character. Maybe that was her goal, who could say.

The smoke-breathing Amazon was Journey's mother, who never stopped moving unless it was to order Journey to stop slouching or to demand a costume change. Whenever she tried to take control, Knox would step in and whisper a few words, which always led to a quiet argument, which stopped everything in its tracks. So Lea found herself with plenty of downtime when she could have been checking her phone, but she tried not to think about it.

Finally, after almost four hours of Knox butting heads with Journey's mother, they somehow came to an agreement that they had what they came for. Lea thanked Journey, who didn't respond as she went back to wardrobe so she could change back into whatever she considered street clothes. Lea and Kathleen started putting away the gear.

It was only after Journey had departed in a scrum of black-suited security men that Knox came over with his Faraday box. He flipped the latch open and held it out so they could retrieve their phones.

"Thanks for cooperating, ladies. I know it can be an inconvenience."

"We understand," Lea said as she retrieved her phone. It took all her willpower not to switch it on immediately. Instead she casually slipped it into her pocket, like a normal human being who didn't need to constantly check her devices. "Thank you for helping out with Mrs. Snow."

He smiled and lowered his voice. "That's not her name."

"You mean Journey Snow is a stage name?" Kathleen asked, faking surprise.

Knox shook his head and chuckled as he walked away. "Mrs. Snodgrass would kill me if I said anything else."

Lea laughed and covered her mouth. Kathleen managed to keep her mask in place longer, but even she had to snicker when they were alone again.

"I guess Journey Snodgrass doesn't have quite the same ring to it, huh?"

"No, it's definitely not a chart-topper," Lea said.

They walked away from the Honeycomb, weighted down with gear. Lea took out her phone and turned it on.

"Wow, couldn't even wait until we were back at the truck, huh?" Kathleen said.

Lea laughed. "Give me a break, I want to check traffic. If it's~" Her phone buzzed and she glanced down at it. Missed call. That made sense, it had been hours. "If it's too crazy we can skip~" The phone buzzed again, then again, and a third time. All missed calls. She frowned down at the screen as the notifications piled on top of each other. Text messages from Janice. More missed calls. Up to sixteen now and still counting.

Her heart felt like it had grown to take up her entire chest, punching against her ribs like a fist. Her hand was shaking so badly that she couldn't even read the screen.

She was vaguely aware of Kathleen moving in close, saying her name, guiding her to one of the decorative stones lining the walkway.

"It's Tori," she finally managed to say. "Something happened to Tori. Tori's hurt."

"What?"

Kathleen looked down at the phone. She took it seconds before Lea's trembling hand would have dropped it to the concrete. She folded her fingers against her palm and leaned forward, hugging herself as her stomach clenched and twisted.

"Something happened to Tori."

Kathleen twisted her head around to look at the screen. "No, babe, almost all these missed calls are from her."

That didn't matter. She couldn't explain why out loud, her words were failing her, but in her heart she knew. The calls came from Tori's phone, it didn't mean she was the one calling. It only meant Annie or the chief had used Tori's phone for some reason. They probably didn't know her number. That made sense. So they got her phone off Tori's body...

She sobbed and put her hand over her eyes.

"Hi, who is this?"

Lea looked at Kathleen. The girl was pale, but there was a steely determination in her eyes. She was holding Lea's phone to her ear.

"I'm Kathleen Abbott, I'm Lea's assistant." A wrinkle appeared between her eyebrows. "What, no, she's fine. She's~" She looked at Lea and held the phone out to her. "It's Tori. She's okay."

Lea sobbed again and grabbed the phone. "Victoria? Are you

okay?"

"Are you okay?" Tori asked at the same time, their voices almost harmonizing. "Where are you, did you get out?"

"Get out?" Lea tucked her hair behind her ears. Her heart had slowed down, but her tears hadn't gotten the all-clear message yet. "What's-what's happening?"

There was a strange choking sound, then rustling as the phone was handed off. Then Janice said, "Lea? You're okay?"

"Rico? What is happening? Why isn't Tori at work?"

"She is." It sounded like Janice was crying as well. "There's a fire at your building. The building with your studio. It's pretty big, apparently, and it took up three floors below yours. No one knew where you were and you weren't answering your phone."

Lea squeezed her eyes shut and growled. "*Ese pinche chamaco* and his fucking Faraday box!"

"What?" Janice said.

"Nothing, I-I-I'll explain later." She took a deep breath and rubbed between her eyebrows. Her head hurt. "Tori's okay?"

"She's fine now. She's been worried sick. But I've been here with her, we've been keeping each other relatively sane."

Lea said, "Okay. Good. I'm glad. Can I talk to her?"

"Sure. But first... Lea..."

"Mm-hmm?"

"*Te amo.*"

She smiled despite the twisting tangle of emotions in her chest. "You do?"

"I do. Tori and I said it to each other earlier. I wanted to say it to you, too."

"*Te amo,* Janice."

More rustling, and then Tori's voice. "Baby?"

"Hi, hi."

"I understand now," she said softly. "I thought I understood before. How you felt. With the not knowing. But I couldn't even imagine. I'm so sorry I tried to fix you o-or~"

"Sh, hey, sh," Lea said. "We don't have to talk about that now. The important thing is that everyone is safe. We can talk tonight. Bring Janice home with you."

"I was planning on it," Tori said.

Lea sniffled. "*Te amo,* Victoria. Goodbye."

"*Te amo,* Lea."

She reluctantly disconnected the call and pressed the phone to her forehead briefly before she dropped her hands. She looked at Kathleen, who was still crouching next to her.

"I chose my confidant very well," Lea said.

Kathleen smiled. "Everyone's okay, I assume?"

"Yes. Just a..." She groaned and waved her hand. "A miscommunication. I'll explain it all on our way back to... *Mierda*. I guess we can't go back to the studio."

"What? Why not?"

"It's on fire."

"*What?*"

Lea waved for her to walk on. "I'll explain at the early dinner I'm taking you to."

"Good enough for me."

Lea stood up and collected the bag she'd dropped when she saw the missed calls. Kathleen waited for her to be situated, and then they started walking back to the parking lot.

Tori sat with her back against the headboard, arms wrapped around her legs, face buried in the crook of her elbow. Janice was sitting next to her, the two of them squeezed together on the twin bed. They'd been lying side-by-side when Lea's call came in. Tori released a tiny, choked sound. Relief tinged with terror. Whatever had happened, good or bad, she was about to get answers, and it had choked her. Tori's hand trembled when she answered, and the tremor passed into her voice when she spoke. And when Lea confirmed she was okay, she'd seen the fear and tension evaporate like the sun had broken through clouds.

She'd been breathing deeply since the call ended. Not crying, but gulping air like she had almost drowned. Janice knew she couldn't say or do anything to help her, so she just sat with her and rubbed her back and shoulder. After a few minutes, Tori lifted her head and started breathing normally again.

"We should tell the others," Janice said quietly. "They seemed just as concerned."

"You're right." She turned her head. "Are my eyes puffy?"

Janice shook her head. She tucked the loose hair behind Tori's ears, then stroked her hand down the back of her head.

"Even if they were, I think they'd all understand. You were worried about your wife."

Tori shook her head and looked away. "I told her to get rid of the app. She just wanted to know what was happening. I can't believe I made her delete it, go to therapy. What was I even trying to fix?"

"You weren't trying to fix her," Janice said. "You were trying to help her cope with the fear. That's all. And now that you've been through the same thing, maybe you can help her better. You know how it feels to be uncertain."

"Six years," Tori said. "She felt this way every time I came to work for *six years*. How did she not go insane?"

"She's tough."

"Yeah, she is."

"And now she has me to share the weight."

Tori held out her hand. Janice took it. "I don't know what I would've done without you today. Thank you for being here for us."

"Hey. We're all in this together." She leaned in and kissed Tori's lips. "I love you both."

"We love you, too," Tori said.

Janice kissed Tori's forehead. "So do you want to go tell the others?"

"Not yet." Tori repositioned herself and put her head down on Janice's chest. "I want you to hold me for a few more minutes."

"Okay," Janice put her arms around Tori and kissed her hair. "We can do that. Just tell me when you're ready."

The fire was put out that night, but Tori predicted the building wouldn't be cleared for the public until the following morning. Lea spent the night with Janice at her apartment, the first time she'd stayed there, and they stayed up most of the night talking and holding each other. They kept Lea's cell phone on the mattress between them. It had become something of a totem to her. She didn't want to let it out of her sight, or risk not waking up if Tori texted during the night.

When Tori's shift ended, the three of them met at Dayton Square and went upstairs together to check out the damage. The fire had been caused by sparks from welders renovating the fifth floor lobby. It had started to spread through the elevator shaft, but the suppression systems kicked in and kept it from creeping too far before the firefighters arrived.

Tori explained that inspectors would spent the next few days making sure everything was still functioning normally, but the structure was sound and it didn't seem to be much chance of another flare-up. Lea was grateful to see that her studio had been spared completely. There wasn't even any stink of smoke because she was far enough from the elevators.

Janice went to the windows and looked out at the part of the lake that could be seen from this position. Lea was in her office making absolutely certain everything was in its proper place. Tori assured her that the firefighters hadn't even come up to the eighth floor, but she wanted to see it all with her own eyes. Tori definitely understood that instinct.

She walked over to join Janice at the glass. "How was she last night?"

"Sleepless," Janice said. "But we both were. You probably figured that out after the tenth text at four in the morning."

"Yeah." Tori smiled.

"We both wish you could've been with us."

Tori nodded. "I wish I was there, too. But once I knew she was out of danger, I couldn't justify it. I was still worried about her, but I couldn't abandon the others."

"I get it. I think she gets it, too. But you may have to teach us how you compartmentalize like that."

"I'll do what I can. Thank you for being there yesterday. For both of us. I don't know what I would've done if you hadn't shown up at the station. And if you hadn't been there to take Lea home..."

"We're both very grateful for you, Rico," Lea said, joining them at the window and standing between them. She stood Tori's hand, then Janice's. "I think yesterday proved that this is going to work. When all the chips were down, we didn't worry about rules or getting anything right. We were just there for each other. I think it worked out well."

"Very well," Tori said.

Janice nodded. "I agree." She squeezed Lea's hand, looking past her at Tori.

"So what do we do now?"

Lea sighed and brought their hands up. She kissed Janice's knuckles, then Tori's.

"Now we figure out everything else."

Chapter Twenty

THREE WEEKS after the Dayton Square fire, Chief Mallory invited everyone from Engine 21 to his house for Thanksgiving. Tori debated what she would say for the entire shift and, on her way out of the station, stopped by his office. She knocked on the open door, and he glanced away from his laptop screen just long enough to confirm who it was.

"Sweet potatoes."

"What?"

He said, "That's what Joan wants you and Lea to bring to Thanksgiving. Sweet potatoes, and she said yams are *not* the same thing. I don't know. But the way she said it made me think it was important."

Tori came into the office. "Okay. Uh, yeah, we can bring sweet potatoes." She was pretty sure Janice would have some idea about how to make it. "Actually, that's not what I was going to say. I just wanted to make sure you and your wife knew that I'm... I'm not, um... I *am* bringing... two. Two guests."

"You got a sister coming into town or something?"

"No. Janice. Our partner." That was the term they'd decided on, after a long debate that had included some godawful candidates she didn't even want to think about.

Mallory finally focused his attention on her. "What do you

mean 'partner'? That lady who came here during that fire at Lea's studio?"

"Right. She and Lea are both coming."

He leaned back in his chair. "I don't know if, uh... if that's the right..." He narrowed his eyes and held up one hand. "Look, Branigan, I don't give a shit what you do behind closed doors. I think it's great you and your wife have such an open and honest relationship. But I've got kids~"

"Your kids are in their twenties, right?"

He pressed on. "I don't think it's necessary to bring along your, your, um..."

"Partner," she said.

"Lea's your partner. She's your wife, right?"

Tori bit the inside of her cheek. "Yes. And we've brought Janice into our relationship."

Mallory muttered under his breath. "Fine. You and your wife have a girlfriend. But I'm not going to explain that to my ki~" He remembered her earlier argument. "Conrad has a ten-year-old. You don't think she's going to be curious? Keep the bedroom stuff in the bedroom. It doesn't need to be dragged out into the open on Thanksgiving."

"Janice is part of my relationship."

"That's great." He gave a weary sigh. "I'm happy you all have your little... throuple."

Tori cringed That was one of the godawful candidates she'd vetoed.

"But," he continued, "it's Thanksgiving. We don't need to make any waves, right?"

"I don't know what to tell you, Chief. But have it your way. I don't want to bring anyone you'd be uncomfortable with. I'm sure Joan will find someone else to bring sweet potatoes."

She started to leave, but he stopped her. "Wait, wait. You're bailing?"

"If you don't want us to bring Janice." She shrugged. "But right now, I don't think she'd want to go anyway. No one likes attending a party if someone had to beg for their invitation. So we'll probably just sit it out."

"You can still come! Joan is fine with you and Lea."

"She's very progressive that way."

Mallory aimed a finger at her. "Hey. Don't do that. This has nothing to do with the fact you're LGBT~"

"Technically I'm only one of those things," she muttered.

"~don't make it about that. If Conrad said 'hey, boss, I want to bring this lady my wife knows from the gym,' I'd be telling him the same thing."

Tori shook her head. "Janice isn't a mistress, or a fling. God, it's been months. We don't sleep with other people."

"Monogamous cheating," he said.

"It's not cheating."

Mallory rubbed his temple with all four fingers. "Jumping Jiminy…"

Tori came into the office and sat down. "Lea and I are in love with Janice. She's in love with us."

"You can't be in love with two people at the same time."

"Of course you can," Tori said. "It happens all the time. Usually people just ignore it or suppress it, but it's not impossible. And if you're open and honest about your feelings, and if everyone involved is mature about it, then it can be a beautiful thing."

Mallory said, "I might get burned alive if you report me for this, but it's just a sex thing, right? You all sleep together?"

"Not that it's any of your business. Yes, we sleep together, but that's implying the whole~"

He cut her off with a wave of his hand. "That's all anyone at Thanksgiving is going to be thinking about. 'This is the lady Branigan and her wife are sleeping with.' They're going to talk about it, and gossip, and make stupid jokes. I just think you would want to avoid all of that. Come to lunch with Lea, have a nice time with the others, catch up with Joan…"

Tori shook her head. "Sorry, Chief. I think Lea and Janice and I will be much happier on our own."

Mallory slumped, defeated. "If you say so. But I just want to be crystal clear, none of us have a problem with you being married to a woman. So get that idea out of your head right now. It's just this idea that you're… that the two of you…" He waved his hand. "I can't ask Joan to just pretend that's normal."

"Okay," Tori said.

"Branigan."

She smiled and held her hands up, surrendering. "I said okay! It's fine. Give my best to Joan."

Tori was almost to the street before Mallory caught up to her. He called her name and she stopped, giving him a chance to catch up.

"You should be in better shape."

"Oh, shut up," he panted.

Tori gestured at herself. "I wasn't even walking fast..."

"I said shut up." He breathed in deeply, hands on hips, and let it out slowly. When he could speak again, he looked at her. "This woman. Janet?"

"Janice."

"You really think of her the same way as Lea? Like... I basically just asked you to not bring your wife to Thanksgiving?"

Tori considered the question. "I don't think it's quite that level yet," she said. "But it was a very similar feeling to my father refusing to invite my girlfriend to my sweet sixteen."

"It's not normal."

"It's *unusual*," she allowed, "but it's actually surprisingly normal at the end of the day."

He nodded skeptically. "The end of the day, when you and Lea both get in bed with the same person, who is... part of your marriage."

"Right."

He shook his head. "I don't get all these loose-y goosy new relationship ideas. I mean, men getting married and women getting married, I get that. I even understood that back when I was a kid. It makes sense. But now you're adding other people and I just don't..." He ran a hand over the top of his head and grunted. "Thanksgiving is about family. And if Janet~"

"*Janice.*"

"~is part of your family, then I'm not going to exclude her. But if this thing falls apart, I don't want you showing up next year with some other couple that you and Lea are swinging with. Understood?"

Tori smiled. "I'll talk to them. See if they're free."

He sighed, clearly relieved. "Good. Fantastic." He turned and started to walk away. "See you Thursday. And don't forget the sweet potatoes, or Joan *will* kick you out, progressive or not."

Lea checked her watch and drummed her fingers on her knee. She looked at Dr. Sherman, who smiled patiently back at her. Lea took a deep breath and looked out the window.

The office was nice. It smelled like some kind of flower. Lea didn't know flowers well enough to identify which one, but it seemed purple. There was abstract art on the walls, and the shelves had books about mental health, spiritual journeys, and healing yourself, all bookended by odd shapes carved out of driftwood or stone.

Lea liked Dr. Sherman. She was nice, and she didn't push too hard. She allowed Lea to say what she wanted to without pushing too hard on the things that weren't ready to come out. She was perfectly fine with sitting in silence until Lea decided what needed to be brought up in the session. Today she was struggling to come up with anything that seemed worthy of bothering a therapist.

"We're spending Thanksgiving with Tori's coworkers," she finally said.

"Oh," Dr. Sherman said. "Is this the first time they'll be meeting Janice?"

Lea shook her head. "They met her after the fire."

Dr. Sherman knew all about the fire. It was what prompted Lea to seek her out, to start testing the waters of returning to therapy. This was their fourth session and so far she didn't want to run for the hills.

"You sound like there's worry involved."

"Sure," Lea said. "The people she work with, they're great people. But they're firefighters. It's very much a, um, boy's club. Even though there's another woman in the company. There were times when Tori still felt uncomfortable talking about being gay, because it was such a big deal that she was a woman. Add gay on top of that, it's a lot. And now she's adding one more non-traditional thing the guys have to accept about her. Tori almost backed out of going entirely because Janice wasn't invited."

"That's a big step. And a big show of support to Janice for how much she means to Tori."

Lea nodded, smiling. "Yes. Janice almost cried when she found out how far Tori was willing to go. I personally wouldn't have been surprised if we skip it entirely on principle. But I know Tori likes her coworkers. Even if she has to push them to respect her and our relationship." She shrugged. "It means a lot to her. So we'll be there."

"To be fair, the three of you have had a few weeks to get accustomed to your new situation," Dr. Sherman said. "Her coworkers haven't had that luxury. It *is* still a lot."

"True. I guess that's true."

"How would you say it's been going?"

Lea's smile widened. "Great. Although I..." She looked down

at her hands, toying with one fingernail. "I feel very selfish sometimes. I feel the need to assure Tori that she's enough on her own. I would be perfectly happy with her a-and I didn't *need* someone else as like a, um... extra thing..."

"Supplemental?"

"Right! Right. That's my concern. I don't want Tori to think I needed more. I would have been perfectly happy with her for the rest of our lives. I knew what I was signing up for, you know? Marriage to her meant that she wouldn't be there half the week. I made the decision that..." She rubbed her lips together and scanned the room as she tried to come up with the right words. "Having her for half the week was better than never having her. I don't think about the times she isn't there. I just appreciate when she *is* there. I wish there was a way I could get that across to her."

Dr. Sherman held out her hand palm-up. "What's wrong with just telling her? The way you told me."

"I... I don't know. I can't just blurt it out like that."

"Sure you can. But if it would make you feel more comfortable, you can build an evening around it. Make her favorite dinner, light some candles, get Janice's favorite wine, and tell them both how much they mean to you. When you first explained this situation to me, you said the key was keeping the lines of communication open. Full honesty. That means being vulnerable. And yes, it takes vulnerability to tell someone how you really feel, even if you're positive how they feel about you in return."

Lea breathed deeply a few times. "Okay. You're right."

"Yes, I am," Dr. Sherman said. "And with that realization, you are officially mentally fit. You've reached the finish line. You're done with therapy."

Lea perked up. "Really?"

Dr. Sherman smiled and tilted her head to the side.

Lea slumped back against the couch. "That was mean. You're going to give me trust issues."

"Something to talk about in the next session, then."

Janice sat in the middle of the bench backseat of Lea's truck with a casserole dish in her lap. She'd gotten Evan to coach her through "the best sweet potato recipe known to humanity" and she was fairly sure she'd managed to do him proud. She was still nervous though. Lea was driving and Tori was in the passenger seat. She hadn't been prepared for how vital seating charts were to Tori.

Personally, Janice didn't care if she was sitting on the outside or between them. She didn't care about being in the backseat. It was a practical decision. Unless Tori wanted to arrive at her chief's house with Janice sitting in her lap, someone had to sit in the backseat.

She *did* mind that it was so cramped, but there was nothing to be done about that. And if she found it cramped, the almost six-foot firefighter would have found it unbearable. So Janice was happy to volunteer.

"Okay, but at dinner you and Lea can sit across from each other."

Janice had just laughed and nodded. "If that will make you happy, then that's what we'll do."

They pulled up outside a condo that already had a small fleet of cars trucks parked along both sides of the street. Lea twisted in the seat and looked at them both.

"So?" She directed the question at Tori. "Are you ready?"

Tori looked up at the house. Then she nodded and looked back at Janice.

"When I came out to them as gay, I did it because there was no way I would ever hide Lea, or pretend I didn't love her as much as I do. I knew how much these people were going to end up meaning to me, and I didn't want to lie to them. I feel the same way now. I want them to know you, Janice. And I want them to know you're not just some woman. You're our partner."

Janice smiled. "Thank you. Both of you. *Te amo.*"

"*Te amo,*" Lea and Janice said together.

They got out of the truck. Tori offered Janice her hand, supporting her while Janice stretched her legs. That backseat was definitely going to be a pain, just not for the reasons Tori was worried about. Once she'd gotten the tingles out of her toes, they started up the front walk. Tori led the way, and Janice fell into step behind her with Lea.

The past few weeks hadn't been easy. The sex helped. She loved being with them both, and being with them separately, and she was surprised at how easily she'd adjusted to the idea of being with a couple. She made dates with Lea to distract her on the days when Tori was at work. When Tori was home, they would either find things all three of them could do together or they would go out together so Lea could have some private time of her own at home. And if Janice needed to step back to focus on the restaurant or just have a night to herself, Lea and Janice found ways to occupy themselves.

She'd expected it to be exhausting. There had been times in the past when just dating one person had been too much of a drain on her. But somehow they'd found a balance. It hadn't been easy. There had been arguments, raised voices, disagreements. So far, though, they'd managed to get through them all without any hurt feelings. She was crossing her fingers that their streak continued.

Tori climbed the steps to the porch, knocked, and stepped back. She looked back at Lea and Janice. She smiled and ducked her chin before looking away again.

Janice wasn't going to lie to herself about their situation. She knew they had a long road ahead of them. There would never be a day when they reached a finish line and said, "Aha, we have done it, we're a fully functioning polyamorous couple!" It was going to be a constant adjustment, they would have to be vigilant not only to their own feelings but to each other's. Lea seemed to be making great progress in therapy. They might look into doing some couples sessions if it wouldn't be a conflict of interest.

The work wasn't done. But the past few weeks had shown they were all ready and willing to do the work, as hard as it might be, to make this thing work. For now, that was enough for her to relax and just enjoy the ride.

The front door to the condo opened and an older woman, presumably Chief Mallory's wife, smiled out at them. She pulled Tori into a hug, said hello to her, and then turned to shout back into the house.

"Andrew! Tori and her partners are here!" She turned back to Tori, motioning them all inside. "Come on, come on. You're right on time."

Tori looked back and then followed Mrs. Mallory inside.

Lea slung her arm across Janice's waist and climbed the steps.

Tori and her partners, she thought with a smile.

It was definitely a title she could get used to.